I0778836

The Housewife Assassin's Doomsday Diary

The Housewife Assassin Series
Book 26

Josie Brown

SIGNAL PRESS

Praise for Josie Brown's Novels

"The last book that made me laugh: *The Housewife Assassin's Handbook.* Brown's unorthodox surprises did make me laugh. I taught it in a class about comic novels."
Jane Smiley, Pulitzer Prize-Winning Author

"On many days, I'll join deep discussions about the works of Le Carré, Deighton, Greene, Ambler, and Forsyth. And then I take incredible delight in a series like *The Housewife Assassin.* Just the name would likely cause eyebrows to be raised, and likely, my stature as an 'expert' falls a bit. Too bad! I read for enjoyment. The authors mentioned above all entertained the heck out of me. And so does Josie Brown's wonderfully fun and amusing series about Donna Stone."
Randall Masteller, *Spy Guys + Gals*

"Brown writes the kind of feminist action plot that men should be reading, especially male authors, to cure that trope of 'vapid sexy girl with a gun.' There's enough comedy sprinkled in between the emotional scenes and within the action to keep readers' minds from going too grim here. As for the sex scenes, these are the best I've ever read. No airy poetry and metaphors. Brown accomplishes setting the mood whether Donna is willing and able or whenever Donna isn't sure what she wants. Brown's hired gun plot is fun, sometimes aggravating, and filled with the wonderful twist of being from a mother's POV."
Amber Love

Novels in The Housewife Assassin Series

Manners, Missiles, and Mayhem (Book 22)

Gambit (Book 23)

Underwater Assets (Book 24)

Deep State Deep Fake Bake-Off (Book 25)

Doomsday Diary (Book 26)

Dear Jack, if you're reading this...

I'm dead, perhaps looking down on you
with all who went before us. As for how, I
will tell you it wasn't pleasant. Should my remains come
your way,
bury me in the spot we always discussed, As for Jeff,
I know
he's taking the news pretty hard. Know that I'll be
sending angels to watch over them all. As for
me, tell the children they will feel me beside them.
To Mary and Trisha, explain that in every
rush of a breeze, they'll feel my presence.
Ah, Jack, Be strong for them! You'll never be alone.
Have heart, my love! I'll always be at your side until
my memory finally fades. In the meantime, please
pretend I'm right there beside you. Even at my
funeral, you will feel is my arms wrap around you,
Watch for signs of me all around you. Kiss the girls
and him for me.

—Your darling Donna

Five Days Ago...

Chapter 1

Survival of the Fittest

The phrase "survival of the fittest" is often misquoted as coming from Charles Darwin as used in his most known tome, originally titled On the Origin of the Species by Means of Natural Selection. *In fact, five years later, another naturalist, Alfred Russel Wallace, suggested to Darwin he replace "natural selection" with something punchier. His advice was "survival of the fittest," which had been coined by the philosopher, Herbert Spencer.*

Instead, Darwin shortened the book's title to Origin of the Species. However, he sprinkled "natural selection" generously within the book.

Ironic, isn't it, that the name of the phrase's originator sank into oblivion—

But not Darwin's.

In that regard, he proved his point.

BUCHANAN CHARLES RANDALL JR.—THE tall silver fox who until recently was the United States Vice President— smiles at me like the cat who's caught the canary. I'm the last in his gauntlet through six interviews at the Madison Project, a prestigious Washington D.C. political think tank. Its white pages are must-reads for practitioners of international diplomacy.

He was gushed upon by all previous interviewers. It won't be happening with me.

You see, I don't really work for this company. Despite this, the Madison Project has kowtowed to the CIA's request that an operative from Acme Industries—the black ops organization I work for—conduct "Two Buck Chuck's" exit interview. (His Harvard frat bros anointed him with this nickname because of the cheap swill he purchased for their house parties, albeit poured into bottles that once held much better wines.)

Politics is a game. If you don't play to win, you might as well go home. The Madison Project's offices reflect their winning streak. Portraits of the heads of state wooed and cultivated by the organization line its hallowed halls. Offices are large and grand enough to make kings jealous. Each one boasts large palladium windows leading out to terraces overlooking a verdant Zen garden where a string trio plays a Chopin prelude. No wonder Two Buck thinks he's a shoo-in for a high-powered, high-profile and sky-high-paying gig that will save his tattered political career.

Wrong. He blew his meteoric ascendancy in our country's current ruling party by aiding and abetting a deepfake video of his boss, President Libby Kentfield. In it, she scorns American citizens after a terrorist attack in which all domestic flights were grounded during Thanksgiving week. To make matters worse, Two Buck then divulged her whereabouts to the saboteurs so that they could blow her up and prop him up as her replacement.

Thanks to Acme, they missed their target.

Because public knowledge of this traitor's deed would irreparably undermine Americans' confidence in our government, Two Buck was given a mere slap on the wrist: the offer to announce he was resigning, ostensibly for family reasons.

Needless to say, running for office again is out of the question, even if the race is for mayor in some backwater town, let alone some truly plum race, like that of a soon-to-be-open Congressional district recently vacated by the addle-minded incumbent who'd held it since the last Cold War. Or, say, relocating to the state of a randy holier-than-thou senator whose very gaudy naughty talks with his on-call hooker du jour was caught on a hot mic.

Two Buck even flirted with the idea of switching parties and running against Libby in the upcoming presidential election. That plan was kiboshed when the opposition party laughed long and hard in his face. It's already got more than its fair share of dirty politicians, thank you very much.

It's said that time heals all wounds. That may be true in politics, but those of us in covert ops live by a different creed. Its driving force:

Payback.

Which is where I come in. Smiling oh so pert and pretty, Two Buck gladly takes me up on my offer to sit. He's even more grateful for the proffered glass of water, having already munched his fair share of the salted pecans from the bowls of the other interviewers' coffee tables: a must-have snack, since the firm lobbies for the nut's trade association.

Little does Two Buck suspect his drink is spiked with a truth serum that will have him spilling his guts as to the who, what, where, when and how he connected with the terrorists.

"Will your wife, Ella, be fine with staying in D.C. after your, um, career change?" I ask.

He opens his mouth to say something but then he pauses. Finally, he murmurs, "She's not so happy about it." Two Buck wipes away a tear.

This sudden bout of honesty is what I've been waiting for. It isn't a heartfelt spousal analysis but proof that Acme's truth serum—Kickapoo Joy Juice—has kicked in.

It's much more accurate than Sodium Pentothal, whose victims' answers are akin to those of a drunk who embellishes his boasts when under the influence of his favorite spirit or varietal.

Acme's Kickapoo Joy Juice does have a serious downside: suspects' psychotic reactions are mixed at best. Whereas men break down in tears, women will verbally attack the interrogator.

I say huzzah to that gender quirk.

(By the way, all Acme operatives must undergo this experience, too. In my case, my sistah solidarity went as far as breaking a chair over my coworker-interrogator's head. I assume my victim—also my boss, Ryan Clancy—hasn't forgiven me because he still ducks whenever I enter his office.)

"My wife is ashamed of me," Two Buck bluntly admits. "I can't say I blame her. I'm pissed at myself too! I really believed them when They told me I'd be the face of a new world order! All I had to do was...was to play along."

"You say 'They.' What are their names?"

He frowns and shakes his head. The question confuses him. "It's no secret who 'They' are. Hell, in politics, They are the source of everything: who is chosen to run, the money that pays for campaigns, the manipulation of the press—and, of course, all means in which the voters are deceived." As he leans back, he closes his eyes. "Those dumb bastard voters..."

Two Buck's head wobbles. Is it because of his anger? Or is it a palsy?

If it's a palsy, is it a side effect of the truth serum?

I tap his cheek with the palm of my hand. "Chuck, be specific. Who are the manipulators? Give me their names."

"Who else would 'They' be? The party is run by those who come with money stuffed in every pocket." Though his eyes are closed, he smirks. "And if a politician is willing to bend over—offer up any and every orifice—and I mean that, figuratively and literally—they're in for a hell of a ride. No matter how hard you kick and scream, the 'They' in question tighten the reins, dig in with their spurs, and don't spare the whip to get where they want—even if it means riding you into the ground."

I chide, "You're talking in metaphors. I want actual names—and I want them *now!*"

He shakes his head. "What you should be asking... is about our ... our... biggest... donorzzz..." By now, he can barely lift his head. "Like....Like the Spen... Spence... be... because... they are...*are doom*...doom..." He slumps down in his chair.

"This is no time to speak in tongues, Two Buck! Be specific!"

Eyes still shut, Two Buck is now gagging.

So that he's lucid once more, I slap his face with my open palm. To keep him from choking, I prop him up.

Bile spews up and out of his mouth—

And onto me, covering me head to toe.

You better believe I'm cussing up a storm. Unfortunately, Two Buck is so afraid of my reaction that he propels himself out of his seat—

And toward the office's open terrace door.

I'm on his heels—

"Heels" being the operative word here. By that, I mean mine. I'm running so quickly that I slip on the marble floor. To stop from tumbling headfirst, I skid on my left one, which breaks, propelling me off kilter but still forward. Instinctively, I grab hold of Two Buck's jacket—

But he's no longer in it. Like a snake, Two Buck has shed it like an old skin. He moves just as quickly—

Toward the terrace's ornate rail—

And then over it: arms spread wide, a gleeful smile on his face, all the while shouting the Harvard fight song.

If you've ever wondered how many of its stanzas can be sung during a twenty-five-story fall, let me assure you, it's not as many as you'd think.

The musicians, hearing it from below, accompany it with the appropriate gusto, never realizing that it isn't a solo from some angel on high, let alone a victory chant from a Madison Project partner, but the funeral dirge of a desperate man—

Whose body falls just a few feet from them.

Instruments now silenced, they stare up at me, horrified. They are wondering if I'm Two Buck's angel of death.

Guilty as charged.

From this height, I doubt they can make out my features. By the time someone summons the police, my Acme team will have covered my tracks. In a fake ambulance and dressed as emergency med techs, my co-mission leader (also my husband) Jack Craig, along with our team's cleaner Abu Nagashahi, will come for the body. At the same time, Arnie Locklear, our tech op, is scrubbing the Madison Project's security feeds of my presence and Two Buck's.

To guarantee that the think tank zips its many lips, its fee will be doubled. But just in case that isn't enough to safe-guard its silence, Emma Honeycutt, Acme's director of Communications Intelligence, will have her team monitor the firm's calls, texts, and emails. A quick perusal of its corre-spondence with its clients should reveal intel that works as blackmail.

None of these fallback positions is ideal, and they are costly.

Ryan will need a fall guy.

Make that a fall gal.

See where I'm going with this?

Time to get back to the office for my walk of shame.

SHITE.

RYAN USUALLY GREETS agents who have screwed the pooch with a snarl bellowed over the intercom demanding that they join him—PRONTO—in the conference room. In my case, he meets me at the elevator door, gets in with me and pushes a button that goes down below the basement level. It isn't lit up, and now I know why: it responds solely to his left eye's scan.

"Chief, I—"

Stopping short, he grabs my wrist. Glaring, he mutters, "Mrs. Craig, I advise you not to say anything until spoken too."

I nod.

I feel the elevator is going down, but since there are no other buttons between that and Acme's garage, all I can do is count the seconds. When I reach forty, my heart jolts along with the elevator, which has finally stopped.

It's only then that I realize I'm still holding Two Buck's jacket. I'm about to point this out to Ryan but then I think better of it. For all I know, this underground lair is Acme's version of a Siberian gulag, and I'll need it for extra warmth.

Slowly, the elevator door creaks open, revealing a long dark hallway. With a firm hand on the center of my back, Ryan steers me out. The hall is so poorly lit that I can't see where it ends.

Each step echoes in the tunnel.

Finally, we reach a stainless-steel door. A biometric security scanner is beside it. Ryan motions me to stand in front of it. After it beeps, the door opens. Immediately after I walk through, a curtain of laser beams shields the door from Ryan's entrance until his eye scan is complete.

The room is circular. I deduce its white shiny wall is also a screen. The only furniture is one chair facing it.

With a nod, Ryan motions for me to take it.

I hesitate a second, just long enough to indulge my instinct to assess a trap door.

None. Foolish me.

I ease onto it.

"Don't try to leave, or you'll be electrocuted," Ryan growls.

To prove his point, he takes a pen from his pocket and tosses it toward the door. When it hits the laser screen, it disintegrates.

Yikes.

He allows his eye to be scanned once more, then walks out.

The door seals with a heavy thunk.

I do the only thing I can:

I wait.

ALMOST TWO HOURS LATER, six chairs, five feet apart, rise from the floor, making a semicircle that faces in the same direction as mine.

With a whisper of suction, the door opens again. Jack, and then Abu, followed by Arnie, come in and that their seats, Emma, right behind them, does the same.

Finally, Ryan enters. The door is just about to shut behind us when our British colleague, Dominic Fleming, breaches the lasers. Though he's in a tuxedo, his tie is undone and his hair is disheveled. A warning siren squeals.

"Bloody hell!" he grumbles. He turns back to face the scanner, but when the laser flashes in his bloodshot eyes, he mutters, "BOLLOCKS!" Still, he stays still until the scan is complete. As he walks through the door, a robotic voice, female, purrs, "Have a nice day...*DOMINIC*."

He replies with a backward two-finger salute, but he's smart enough to keep quiet under Ryan's warning glare.

"Why didn't he disintegrate?" I ask.

Ryan's chair swivels in my direction. Catching my eye, he mutters, "Because unlike you, Mrs. Craig, he didn't blow a mission." His head whips around to Dominic. "I'm sure that day will come."

Lips zipped, Dominic stares straight ahead.

Ryan's glare shuts me up. I purse my lips to stay serious and silent.

In time, our boss declares, "Gentlemen, were you able to cover Mrs. Craig's tracks?"

"The Madison Project knows that mum's the word," Jack replies, "Otherwise, whatever the CIA has on it will torpedo its relationship with its less-than-reputable clients."

"We owe Marcus for that. No doubt his ounce of flesh will be considerable." Ryan's nod toward me comes with a scowl. I imagine he's wondering if my head on a spike will appease DNI Branham.

"Where's Randall's body?" he asks.

"Several leagues under the sea, off the coast of Long Beach," Abu replies. "His yacht sank quickly enough, as would be the case when the bilge door is left open. He'll be shark chum soon enough."

We wiped his calendar and his computer's cloud of any mention of the Madison Project," Jack adds.

"I left a suicide note in the cabin," Arnie adds.

"Since his wife left him and his political connections

were burned when Libby dropped him, it'll track as a suicide," I acknowledge.

"That certainly works in our favor," Ryan admits.

"Sir, DNI Branham's aide is linking us through," Emma warns.

A few seconds later, the screen is live.

Director of Intelligence Marcus Branham appears. Though his demeanor is calm, he looks more tired than I've ever seen him. He allows himself a slight smile and a nod. "Ryan, thank you for facilitating my hasty request for this meeting. And Donna, it's good to see you again."

Relieved, I grin. "You too, sir." *Well, well, well! This isn't so bad after all...*

As if reading my mind, Ryan murmurs, "Don't get too cocky."

I acknowledge his warning with a slight nod.

"Time is of the essence, so I'll get on with the details of the mission, which I now entrust to Acme, and solely to the team assembled before me," Marcus declares. "Chuck Randall verified what we already suspected: that Libby's party is compromised by Russian spies."

"You mean to say he wasn't their only asset in Libby's political party?" Jack asks.

"Affirmative," Marcus replies. "This Acme team is tasked with rooting out the other saboteurs. We do have leads, however." Worry etches his brow. "It hasn't yet been announced that the tech billionaire Aiden Spencer and his wife, Ruby, were killed last night when their private jet crashed into the Swiss Alps. Their personal staff, who always fly with them, also perished. They were heading to their Palo Alto estate from their penthouse in D.C. The disaster caused an avalanche, which buried the plane. It may not be found for years, if at all."

Jaws drop at the stunning news.

"It's no secret the couple were notoriously private—so much so that no one has ever seen them," Marcus points out.

"Do you mean in person?" I ask.

"Yes. And there are no photos anywhere either," Marcus explains. "All their correspondence was handled electronically through an instant messaging platform Aiden developed specifically for his private use. The few conversations the Spencers had were always via mobile. Even their few domestic and corporate staffs received their orders sight unseen."

"Talk about keeping below the radar!" Abu declares.

"Considering their wealth and status, why would they opt to be modern day Greta Garbos?" Dominic muses.

Abu snorts. "Maybe it has something to do with all the handouts requested of the world's third richest man."

"What exactly do we know about the Spencers?" Jack asks.

"Not much," Emma admits. With a flick of a finger, pages from the couple's dossiers align on the screen. "Ruby was British. They met when she was at university in Paris— an art major."

"To be expected, considering she graduated from the Sorbonne. From the dossier, I see they were collectors: impressionists and modern masters—not that anyone got to see their acquisitions, what with their reclusive natures," Dominic grouses.

"Yes...but all of her classes were independent study," Emma points out. "The *New York Times Magazine*'s so-called profile on Ruby is so thin that it could have been mistaken for a *People* article—you know, cobbled together from rumors, hearsay, and social media. "

"Let me guess. Aiden's is just as thin," Abu declares.

"Affirmative," Marcus admits. "He was American and considered a tech savant. Although he was accepted to six universities—Harvard, Yale, and Stanford included—he elected to skip school altogether. In the one interview he had with *Wired,* he claimed it would be a waste of his time. Considering the patents already held in his name and the money they made, he was right."

Perplexed, I shake my head. "Am I to deduce that there are no pictures of the Spencers anywhere?"

"Correct. And, frankly, this works in our favor," Marcus declares.

"How so?" I ask.

"Because you, Mrs. Craig, along with Mr. Craig, are to take their places," Marcus explains.

Jack's eyes meet mine. He's just as stunned as me.

Chapter 2

Doomsday

*I*n general, the word "doomsday" describes a time of catastrophic destruction and death. However, another term, even more specific is, "the day of final judgement." Do they mean the same thing?

Not really. Here's how to make the distinction between them:

What causes catastrophe, destruction and death? Well, that depends. Holy wars? Great example. Nuclear war? Certainly! Epidemics with no medical cures? For sure. Humankind's history is littered with such waste of time, effort, less than noble causes, and lost lives.

If one were to define "the Day of Judgement," an era of floods, famine, fire, and damnation would be involved. Each is just as Biblical in its causes as in its aftermath.

So, who is it assumed will be saved? Only those deemed innocent.

And who are these innocents?

Well, certainly not YOU.

Remember what The Good Book says: "Let he who is without sin cast the first stone."

In other words, when all Hell breaks loose, you had better duck and cover like the rest of us.

"LET ME GET THIS STRAIGHT," Jack declares. "Donna and I supposed to pass ourselves off as the richest couple in the world? Just how do you figure we'll pull it off?"

"By staying incognito, the Spencers made it easy for you," Marcus insists. "But unlike Aiden and Ruby, you'll do what they never did: agree to meet with those politicians who have begged for private audiences."

"They'll be the belles of the ball. Every politician, both parties, will come hat in hand to curry the Spencers' financial support," Abu points out. "And they'll do anything asked to get it."

"Wait a minute!" I exclaim. "I think Two Buck mentioned them in his interrogation."

"Emma, please scan the video," Ryan commands. "If Donna is correct, play the passage for us."

"On it, boss," she replies.

A moment later, the video appears on the screen. Two Buck shivers as if palsied.

"What you should be asking... is about our ... our... biggest... donorzzz... Like....Like the Spen... Spence... be... because... they are...are doom...doom..." **He then slumps down into his seat.**

"Talk about prescient!" Arnie exclaims. "He actually predicted they were doomed!"

"There's no way he would have known about the crash," I point out. "Am I right about the timing?"

Since it happened after he fell to his death, doubtful," Dominic affirms.

"Two Buck's revelation matches the chatter the CIA intercepted from the Russians about the Spencers." Marcus explains. "Specifically, that Aiden created a Doomsday device."

The news stuns my team into silence.

"Are they blackmailing the U.S. to keep the device off the market?" Abu asks.

"Not exactly," Marcus replies. "If they were, they'd have reached out to POTUS. Instead, they've contacted members of both U.S. political parties who the CIA has long suspected are Russian assets."

"Why use Russia as the middleman?" I ask.

My best guess: it would allow the Spencers to walk away with a large payday and still stay invisible. But since no one else knows they're dead, Acme's mission is to catch these stateside saboteurs in the act."

"These Russian assets would have also been behind the recent attack on Libby over Thanksgiving," I reason. "Two Buck was merely the bomb's courier."

"My thoughts exactly." Marcus grows larger on the screen as he leans in. "Acme, your mission is to prove or disavow this premise—*no matter where it takes you*. To be clear: this is an off-the-books op. And considering how important it is to protect POTUS physically, she is to have no knowledge of it—nor anyone else on her team."

This is Marcus's delicate way of informing us that should the op go sideways, he can't cover our asses.

"In other words, we're to initiate ghost protocol," Ryan clarifies.

Though awed by this revelation, everyone mutters, "Affirmative."

"Whether their payday was to come from Russia, China, or the U.S., how much were the Spencers asking for their Doomsday device?" Jack asks.

"You'll get your answer from these four suspected Russian assets." Marcus taps his console.

The screen morphs into two photos. One is a very tall and handsome man in his late-forties. He's blond and blue-eyed, as is his wife and two very young children: a boy and a girl.

"As you already know, this is the opposition party's presidential frontrunner: Senator Broderick Page," Marcus says. "Page has represented Florida for almost a decade. Before that, he served two terms in Congress. He went to college on a basketball scholarship. He married his high school sweetheart, Jenny, and plays up the family man angle to the hilt."

"A true-blue husband? Finally," Jack mutters.

"Hardly!" Marcus admits. "He makes no bones that he's open to liaisons."

"Then Donna is to play honeypot." Jack's monotone reflects his disapproval that this is a foregone conclusion.

I'm upset too. No better time to get both our minds off this reality: "Why is that not any worse than Libby's single status? The opposition finds any excuse to rub her nose in it."

"Yet another reason why Page was their ideal candidate —until Libby chose Lee as her running mate," Marcus explains. "Lee's pending nuptials even the playing field, not to mention the public loved Lee when he was POTUS."

Jack rolls his eyes. Lee recently made a formal announcement about his engagement to his assistant, Eve Green. But it was only after Jack heard me tell Lee that the only man I love is the one I married that he was convinced Lee finally got the message.

About damn time.

Another photo appears on the screen. No joke: she's got the body and face of a Barbie doll.

As if reading my mind, Emma mutters, "Her plastic surgeon certainly pulled out all stops!"

"Kellie Diller is the opposition party's chairperson. Because she always wears pink, the press has dubbed her 'The Pink Lady," Marcus explains. "But she's much more lethal than the cocktail. In fact, her nickname among lobbyists is 'Killer Diller,' for good reason: she's the ultimate political wheeler-dealer and not above arm-twisting—let alone blackmail—to get elected officials to toe the party line. Rumor has it that a California congressman who stubbornly refused to vote her way was stupid enough to go on a deepsea fishing trip with her—and never came back. The man's widow denies the trip ever happened. She claims he passed in his sleep. But because it was a closed-coffin funeral, no one knows for sure. What is certain is that the widow took over his term in office with Kellie's blessing. Lo and behold, her votes have never deviated from Kellie's orders."

"In other words, all party members do so—or else they won't be the party's Chosen One," I say.

"Unsurprisingly, Kellie is not above using sex to get her way," Ryan declares. "As, we're sure, Jack will find out."

My husband stares at the ceiling. He doesn't need to study her face. He'll see enough of it —and every other inch of her—on this mission.

"As you'd imagine, Libby's party is also courting the Spencers," Marcus explains. "Senator Wilbur Lassiter, from Virginia, and Congresswoman Gabriella Calloway, based in Silicon Valley, are the majority leaders in POTUS's party. Because of their senior positions in their respective houses, Lassiter and Calloway also head up the President's campaign fundraising committee. In that capacity, they interface with deep-pocket donors. To add credence to why either—or both—could be beholding to Russia, they're not above feathering their own PACs with a slice of what comes in as donations. If they are indeed compromised, they can lead us to the funnel for Russian dark money. Donna and Jack, you're to get as close to them as possible in, er, every sense of the word."

Again, Jack frowns. He's as dismayed as me.

"By the way, you should make it clear to POTUS's emissaries—who, we presume will be Wilbur and Gabriella—that she's already on your list to receive a generous donation, so there is no need for her to show up to kiss your rings. That way, we avoid having her—or, for that matter, Lee—unwittingly blow your covers."

"A break from Lee is also fine with us," Jack declares.

"If I hear that Libby's team has suggested he reach out, I'll discourage it," Marcus assures us. "The Spencers' notorious love of privacy is something Lee can certainly relate to."

"Frankly, I'm still surprised he threw his hat back into the ring," Emma says.

"He feels he owes it to his country." Ryan replies. "As for the rest of your team, Abu will act as your chauffeur. Dominic, your cover is that of the Spencers' butler, and—"

"*I beg your pardon?*" Dominic's stentorian declaration would encourage a Shakespearean acting company to hire him on the spot. "Merely a *butler*? I am MIFFED!... No, no —that doesn't do justice to my feelings—let alone my social standing!" He rises. "I am fuming! Livid!... *GUTTED*."

Ryan sighs. "Okay, then. You'll be the Spencers' personal concierge."

Dominic frowns. "A rose by any other name—"

"Unless you'd prefer to be their chauffeur." Taking note of our boss's tone, Dominic halts his rant.

Ryan shrugs. "I thought not."

Dominic's lower lip is quivering. Too bad. At the very least, in his bespoke suits, I bet he'll be the best-dressed personal concierge on the block.

"Now, regarding where you're to entertain your callers: the Spencers own three residences," Marcus continues. "While in D.C., you have a condominium at the Watergate. It's in the 2700 building, Unit 2720. For your convenience, unless otherwise notified, dead drops will take place in its mailbox."

"Noted," I respond.

"The Spencers also own an oceanside mansion in Palm Beach and an estate in Silicon Valley's Palo Alto, which sits on six square acres. This mission calls for the Acme team to spend time at all three homes"—Ryan explains—"which is where Arnie comes in. Aiden's IT apparatus is in hidden rooms within each home. You won't just be hacking a hard drive but an entire server farm. Unfortunately, since the Spencers' plane wreckage has yet to be recovered, we don't have the body parts necessary to breach his state-of-the-art security measures such as eyes for scanning, or fingers for prints, let alone photos to reconstruct their heads for facial recognition access. You'll live in those rooms until the farms are hacked."

Arnie high-fives one hand with another. "That's fine with me! It sure beats being yet another lackey to the Craigs —er, *Spencers*. Best of all, I get to eat where I sleep! Emma forbids that. You know, crumbs and all."

Embarrassed, his wife slaps her forehead.

Arnie apologizes with a shrug. "Sorry, babe! Just speaking truth to power."

As Ryan groans, Marcus adds, "Craigs, feel free to make those who come hat-in-hand go out of their way to do so. In fact, they'll expect it."

"Palm Beach sounds brill! At least I can work on my tan," Dominic admits.

"The Florida sun is hotter than you're used to," I warn him.

"I beg to differ!" he sniffs. "My numerous stays in the Virgin Isles lend credence."

Pointedly, Marcus barks, "Moving on, folks, to the biggest reality of this mission: you'll play the long game. It's the only way to identify possible saboteurs before they can act." He scans the screen, making eye contact with each of us.

Besides missing Trisha and Jeff, leaving them with Aunt Phyllis for all that time may drive them crazy, especially if her husband, Porter Crosby, hits the road with Lee. As part of his Secret Service detail, the odds are great.

Our poor kids.

What I do for my country deserves a medal—for them as well as me.

I sigh. "So, the sooner we find the moles, the quicker I get back to being little ol' me."

"Exactly," Marcus replies. "Which brings us to our final suspect in Libby's party." A man's photo appears on the screen: mid-fifties, balding, a slight belly. "One who is sure to come calling on the Spencers is Libby's campaign manager, Tommy Jensen. He's had that role in every campaign since she was the junior congressperson from Wisconsin's second congressional district."

"Libby calls him the brother she never had," I remind him.

"That's because he'll do anything for her. He lost a finger to frostbite because he was knocking on doors during a snowstorm."

"Blimey! Talk about devotion," Dominic whispers.

I ask, "Why is he a possible suspect?"

"Considering Russia's success with kompromat, we can't overlook the campaign staffer closest to Libby," Marcus reminds us.

"A word of warning," Ryan adds. "Should Libby lose the election—or worse yet, should you fail in protecting her—it goes without saying that the mission's status also safeguards any immediate successors from backlash."

In other words, the winning candidate will not be read in about our mission since he or she will probably go ballistic, particularly if we've crossed a line considered criminal in the eyes of the law.

Or worse still, if we've uncovered her successor's dirty tricks against Libby.

"Once proof of their treason has been established, how should Acme proceed?" I ask.

"That depends," Marcus replies. "None are viable double agent candidates. That said, ideally, the suspect will not be aware that his or her cover is blown until they are arrested. Otherwise, they'll attempt to leave the country as opposed to being tried for treason." He sighs. "To put it bluntly, if any proven suspects resists arrest, I leave their fates to Acme's discretion."

In other words, exterminate—but make it look like an accident or natural causes.

I shrug. "Gotcha."

"I guess that's it in a nutshell..." With Marcus's hesitation comes a stare—directly at me. "Donna, what's that in your hand?"

"Oh!... It's Two Buck Randall's jacket." I grimace. "I posed as his job interviewer at a think tank. After taking Acme's truth serum, he, um... Well... it was the only thing I could hold onto before he took his swan dive off the balcony."

Marcus nods slowly. "If I remember correctly, this isn't the first time that this particular concoction has had a fatal effect."

Ryan frowns. "We're still tweaking the formula."

Marcus shakes his head. "Perhaps it's time to dispose of it, once and for all."

"Acme will take that into consideration, sir," Ryan declares.

Doubtful, but I know better than to muse this aloud.

"I take it that nothing in Randall's pockets—or for that matter, his wallet–provided any useful intel?" Marcus asks.

Ryan and I exchange looks. He's deduced rightly that I haven't looked through them.

Then again, he hasn't either.

"Donna just walked in the door when your call came through. We'll get on it right away," Ryan assures him.

"Call me if there's good news. I could use some." He signs off.

"Couldn't we all," I murmur.

I open the jacket's right pocket. Two Buck's wallet is in it.

Before taking it, Ryan pulls his kerchief from his jacket pocket. Using it as a makeshift glove, he rifles through it. There is Two Buck's driver's license (its photo is obviously from a decade prior); a rolled condom (in case he got lucky between trysts with his various mistresses. He had a wife, but they've had an "arrangement" since she caught him *in flagrante delicto* with one of his aides); and several exclusive credit cards, including one from Dubai First Royale.

Ryan nods grudgingly. "At least this gives us a head start on following the money."

I open the coat's other pocket. It seems empty—

But no, there something in there: a business card for a coffee shop that was within walking distance of the Madison Project's office building. A few numbers and letters are scribbled on the back.

Ryan picks it up with the kerchief, then scans it. "This looks like a code. Emma, take it to Acme Forensics. See if they can lift any prints other than Randall's and now yours. Afterward, one of our codebreakers will take a crack at it. As for Randall's coffeeshop meeting: Arnie, check out any CCTV in the shop or the surrounding blocks to see if we can find out Randall's contact." Ryan glances around the room. "Folks, go home and pack your go-bags. Your flight is wheels-up at midnight."

Already I hate this assignment.

Chapter 3

Prepper

In Doomsday parlance, a "prepper" is someone who insists that the collapse of Earth's civilization is inevitable and prepares for it.

Every generation has its fair share of preppers. In prehistoric times, the cave dwellers' paintings of their vision of The End may seem rudimentary now, but Noah's Ark proved them right. In the 1620s, Martin Luther was burned at the stake for harshing Henry the 8th's mellow with the topic.

Bomb shelters can still be found beneath homes built between the early 1950s and 1960s. Should you buy one, I dare you to open one of its many cans of Spam and declare it digestible.

(I'd have said the same thing the day it was put down there, so, really nothing has changed.)

Ask any prepper you meet if it's worth it. My guess: you'll get the same answer any Cub Scout would give: "It never hurts to be prepared."

And then there's Horatio's school of thought: "Carpe diem quam minimum credula postero." Loosely as opposed to literally translated, it means "Live in the present without worrying about tomorrow."

In other words, why choose your poison when it's less stressful to wait for it to find you?

I'M NOT surprised at all that when we break the news to Jeff and Trisha about our business trip, their response is dead silence and disappointed stares.

Suddenly, Trisha groans. "Oh, heck! Janie is going out of town too. But...I guess we'll have to get used to that, now that her father is President Kentfield's running mate."

"I'm so sorry, kiddos. We'll do our best to get back to you as soon as possible." I pray they don't hear the catch in my throat. "We'll call every day. Promise."

"So...you'll be together?" Jeff watches us closely for our response.

"Some of the time, but not always," Jack says.

"Will you be with the Chiffrays?" Jeff asks.

"Your mother will." Jack's answer is matter of fact. And yet, Jeff's response is a frown.

Jack sees it too. "Why do you ask?"

"Just getting the lay of the land." Jeff realizes our assignment could be dangerous—not just for us, but for Lee and Janie too.

He's worried for Janie.

"Not to worry," Jack assures him. "All in a day's work."

"They'll be on the road a long time," Trisha counters. "According to Aunt Phyllis, she may not see Porter for a month! Will you be gone that long too?"

Our children catch the glance between Jack and me.

Jeff groans. "Really? You'll be away that long?"

"Which means we'll be left with Aunt Phyllis all that time, too!" Trisha adds.

"But you love her!" I point out.

"In small doses," Jeff declares.

"Mary comes home from U.C. Berkeley on weekends," Jack reminds them.

"To be with Evan, not with us," Trisha argues.

Though it may be true that our eldest now practically lives at her fiancés house, I'm not going to allow our children to use that as an excuse to guilt-trip us into staying.

My guilt is great enough as it is.

I throw up my hands. "I'll ask her to make you her priority, okay? I promise."

"Whatever." Trisha's eye roll makes her point.

Jeff dismisses us by turning his back.

Despite this, I hug him and pull Trisha into it too.

Jack's arms go around all of us.

Usually, our kids squirm at drawn out shows of affection. Not today. We've yet to walk out the door and already they miss us.

I miss them too.

———

AN HOUR BEFORE TAKE-OFF, one of Acme's limos picks us up from the firm's underground parking lot to take us to Van

Nuys Airport. It pulls into a private terminal so that no one sees us exit the car and enter Acme's Gulf Stream 700.

After the mission, we'll follow the same protocol: each operative will leave in a different limo so that we arrive separately at Acme headquarters for our debriefing.

Our pilot, George Taylor, is waiting for us beside the air stairs along with his co-pilot, Jessica Berry. As the mission leaders, we rate the cabin's private bedroom.

With the awful day I've had, the second my head hits the pillow, I take it for granted that I'll quickly fall asleep.

Wrong. Jack's arms wrapped around me coupled with the knowledge that this mission may take longer than normal makes me hold onto him and never let him go. His head is buried in my hair. I hear him inhale deeply and sigh longingly. I know he is hard with lust; I feel him against me.

I turn to face him and stroke his cheek. He leans in for a kiss. When our mouths meet, our passion revives us. Or perhaps it's the realization that hurtling through the air some thirty-six thousand feet over the Earth at four hundred miles an hour shortens what little time we have together with each second that passes.

We can't waste a minute. Soon it will be showtime, and all that implies.

Once again, our wits must be sharply honed. In a blink of an eye, we'll be forced to make life or death decisions. If needed, we will use all weapons at our disposal. Not just guns, knives, or bombs, but our bodies too.

When in bed with a target, I'd prefer to slit his neck than to kiss it. One hand may taunt his penis with gentle strokes. But I must stifle the urge to stab his heart with the stiletto in the other.

Make no mistake: I'm not a traitor to my marriage. My marks are Judases to our country.

Jack brings me back to the here and now. He rises over me. I guide him into me. His thrusts may set the rhythm for our torrid tango, but my clenches direct the steps for this mutual journey through the ballroom of emotions that await us. The analogy is apt, for where else do we find pain so pleasurable than in the arms of the one person with whom we glide through each emotion—longing and lust; the agony of anticipation; the ecstasy of climax—as if it's yet another practiced dance step?

Who else takes me higher and reads my every move, up until climax?

It's why we are partners.

As with dancing, when it comes to lovemaking, practice makes perfect.

Yes, we should be sleeping. But you know what they say: you'll have plenty of time for that when you die.

Or, in our case, when the mission is over.

If we're still alive.

WHEN WE LAND, the limo to take us to the Watergate is waiting inside a Dulles Airport private terminal. Abu takes the driver's seat and Dominic rides shotgun while Jack and I wait in the back for the coded message from Arnie that he's hacked the electronic lock on the Spencers' condominium. Before we arrive, he will secure a retinal scanner already loaded with the eye prints of all our team members so that we can come and go as we please.

Abu is waiting outside with coded key cards that allow us entrée into all the Watergate office and residential buildings as well as their parking lots. He's even got a copy of the mailbox key.

"I initiated facial recognition ghost blocks for the whole mission team," he informs us. "That way, no matter where Abu, Jack, Dominic, you, or I go, no one can track us."

"That's a relief," I admit.

Our new digs are even more sumptuous than I'd imagined. Dominic marvels at the kitchen appliances, the pristine surfaces in all the private spaces ("Six bathrooms! Eight bedrooms! The formal dining room can seat twenty! A study to rival the British Library!"), and the views from every room.

I agree, they are truly spectacular.

It takes Arnie an hour, but he's found the room holding the control center for the abode's neural network. It is hidden behind a wall in the library. What with all its state-of-the-art technological amenities, Arnie is in his Valhalla. Though security visuals of all rooms are one of its key features and surface-touch commands are another. Its screens are an ever-morphing photo montage from one room to another.

Arnie points out one specific virtual reality feature. "It's the latest, greatest, and has not yet even been released!"

"Why are you whispering?" I ask.

"I dunno. I guess... It's because his place is spooky." Arnie shivers. "It almost feels as if it is listening to us."

I raise a brow. "If you're too spooked to work down here, maybe we should get another tech op to keep you company."

"No! Not at all... I mean...I know it's silly." He shrugs. "Just don't forget I'm down here, okay?"

"Never. In fact, in that to-die-for kitchen, I'll whip up a

batch of cherry tartlets just for you, and come down here to drop them off. Every day, with coffee," I vow.

Arnie's face lights up. "You're on! And I'll do my best to hack this farm in record time." He pats his belly. "Your tarts will be a great incentive. Just don't tell Emma. I promised her I wouldn't gain weight on this trip."

Arnie pats the side of one of the servers—

But then he lifts his hand and shakes it, all the while cussing up a storm.

"What's wrong?" I ask.

"It's as hot as a stove!" Arnie frowns. "I'll need to turn up the air conditioning. Otherwise, this whole room will blow sky high."

I grimace. "You'd better get on it. In the meantime, I'll send Jack, Abu, and Dominic for portable fans. The sooner the better, because it may be the same in their Palm Beach and Palo Alto homes."

Though wincing, he nods.

Forget the tartlets. I'll bring him a whole pie. Should it take him longer than expected to fix the issue, at least it will never get cold.

As I ENTER the living room, Jack lights up. "Abu, tell Donna your idea."

"I'm all ears." To prove it, instead of sitting beside Jack, I flop down beside him on the humongous sectional sofa ensemble: Roche Bobois' latest version of its classic Mah Jong design.

"Since every PAC, lobbyist, and politician in town has

been courting the Spencers, why not throw a cocktail party and invite them all?" Abu suggests. "The caveat is that they won't be admitted unless they first relinquish their mobile devices. While they hobnob with you, Arnie, Dominic, and I will hack the devices and scan their SIM cards so that we can assess them later for suspicious activity."

"Brilliant," I say in my poshest British accent. "Then we'd better get the invitations out as soon as possible."

I'm chuffed when Dominic gives me an approving nod.

"On it," Emma assures us via our earbuds. "Mr. and Mrs. Spencer, we need to get your wardrobes up to snuff as soon as possible. We're in luck! Three of Jody Keleske's social media clients are clothing designers. Fashion Week just ended in New York. She was there, holding their hands. I asked her to pull together some ensembles that will at least get you through the next week. The Acme plane that got you to D.C. has picked her up. Her D.C. event planners can set up while she dresses you. I asked her to hang there for the party to supervise the photographers, and to post photos on social media. I'm sure the campaign aides of those in attendance will also be reposting on their boss's S.M. feeds."

"The first party's invitations will go to the best financed members of the opposition party and its party chair." Jack snaps his fingers at Dominic. "Butler, please reach out to their offices via email with the appropriate invitation. We'll do the same with Libby's party the following night."

"If it is to indeed be appropriate, I'd suggest a printed invitation, hand-delivered, and received with a signature by the invitee's highest-ranking aide," Dominic says.

"Excellent suggestion," Jack declares. "Hand deliveries it is."

Dominic's smile is now wide and glorious. But then it falls flatter than a pancake.

I nudge him. "What's wrong?"

He turns red. "I'm... Well, I'm Jody's knight in shining armor. I'd hate her to see me as a lowly butler."

He's well aware he must prove he still deserves a place in our mutual pal's heart, especially now that she's aware he is also seeing Teddy Twala, an MI6 operative. The women's paths crossed at my Thanksgiving dinner table.

"Well, then, congratulations! Since you've saved us from making our first faux pas, I'm promoting you to Mr. and Mrs. Spencer's quote-unquote private secretary."

"A cracking idea!" I exclaim.

This time, Dominic winces. "I say, madam! That sounded a bit naff. We'll need to work on your delivery. Not to worry! We'll have you tickety-boo in no time."

"Good," I reply. "Then, when Jody arrives with the invitations, you, Arnie, and Abu can coordinate their hand deliveries."

"I can help with that," Jack insists. "It sure beats sitting around in a monkey suit until the party starts."

Dominic stands up. "Then we should begin post haste. Shall we retire to the library?"

BY THE TIME Jody has arrived with the invitations, my accent passes muster. The rest of our mission team, Jack included, leave to make the hand deliveries.

Because no one knows what the Spencers look like, Abu has altered Jack and my appearances. Jack's bottle green eyes are now brown. Mine, previously gray, are also brown. As for Jack's hair, it's now blond and mostly shaved except for a spiked crown. His brows are also blond. He hasn't shaved, so there is visible scruff. His nose is slightly crooked.

My hair, a wig, is now a sleek bright red bob. I don't know how he did it, but Abu gave me a scattering of freckles on my nose. My lips are also fuller.

I'm also wearing a retainer that gives me a slight overbite. Jack nods approvingly. "That's certainly sexy."

"The Tudors thought so as well," Dominic informs us. "It was the common feature of the era's saucy wench— emphasis on 'common.'"

I shake a finger at him. "You prat! You're already holding it against me."

Jody has brought a tuxedoed battalion with her. After shaking Jack and my hands, she acknowledges us as Mrs. Spencer and Mr. Spencer, and then off she goes with her minions. Their carts are laden with the typical party apparatus: a variety of cocktail glasses and bottles filled with various spirits, fine china, heavy silverware, and expensive linens. Besides crates of various top-brand liquors, kegs of artisan beers, and expensive wine varietals, there are bins filled with food that will be grilled, cooked, or sautéed and then chopped, diced, or sliced into tempting tidbits laid out on the silver trays to proffer our esteemed guests. As Jody strides through each room, they march behind her, taking note of her commands, acknowledging their roles in her strategy, and breaking off to set up their stations.

Jody points to a specific place in the enormous living room. "This is where a jazz trio and the singer are to set up," she explains.

"Acme operatives all," Emma informs us. "Their amplifiers double as recording devices. My COMINT team will analyze all conversations. Any that are relevant to the mission will be used as evidence."

"Excellent idea," I reply.

Jody accompanies me to the master bedroom. There, two of her staff have already filled its closets with Jack and my new wardrobes. As I shower, Jody pulls out several long gowns for me to try on.

All the dresses are stunning. The one that both Jody and I feel is the perfect choice is a gown from the couturier Carolina Herrera. Its sex appeal comes from its trifecta of color, contour, and cut. A candy-apple red slim straight body-skimming skirt is attached above my navel to a sweet pink long-sleeved rounded-neck top, leaving the rest of my waist exposed. A long black sash, tied in a bow at the nape of my neck, hangs down my bare back. I choose pink heels over red ones. My only jewelry are dangly ruby earrings.

Jack, now back from hand-delivering the invitations, catches my eye in the octagonal dressing room's mirrored walls and whistles. "If this were just a two-person party, I'd already have you out of that get-up."

"Hold that thought until later tonight, after all our guests and staff are gone. In the meantime, while Jody's team does my hair and make-up, take your shower and put on the tux that Jody picked out for you."

"Don't forget we have to do this all over again tomorrow night with Libby's political party," he reminds me.

I lean my head on Jack's shoulder. "I can get used to this life."

"Well, don't. We're playing a game of cat and mouse," he

reminds me. "And, unfortunately, we're the prey. We can never forget that."

He's right. Still, a girl can dream, right?

Chapter 4

Judgement Day

Various theologies believe that the end of the world coincides with God's judgment of humankind.

However, Isaiah 30:18 in the King James Bible puts the kibosh on the "wrathful God" theory this way: "Therefore, the Lord waits to be gracious to you; therefore, he will rise up to show mercy to you."

And all these years, you thought only your mother's opinion counted. Tell me you're relieved!

WE—THAT is, the Spencers—are the talk of the Watergate.

Despite the impromptu invitations, many of our distinguished and well-connected neighbors have readily RSVP'd. Having hacked the building's security cameras, our mission team takes note that the Watergate has been abuzz since the invitations went out. Considering that no one has ever seen the real couple, let alone met them, those with the invitations are pleased as punch.

As the throngs hit the elevator banks, those tenants who weren't invited are calling down to the lobby concierge to find out who's throwing the shindig. Despite never having met the Spencers—then again, who has?—it seems these folks are miffed that they didn't make the cut.

They should be glad. Better not to be a terrorist suspect.

As our guests enter the Spencers' grand entrance, the security team— Abu, Arnie, and Dominic—relinquishes them of any errant electronic devices before they are allowed to make their way to us.

Guided by Emma's softly whispered reconnaissance, Jack and I greet them warmly with a personal aside that serves as an ice breaker, and a manufactured memory of where our paths almost crossed. Sometimes it's a seemingly observant tidbit that exudes genuine interest in some special corner of their private lives. Or perhaps it's a little-known fact of a charity they support. If the guest is a politician, it's a shoutout about a bill they sponsored. Their surprise at our interest seems real, more so because it isn't expected.

They are taken aback because they should be wooing us, not the other way around. Thrown off kilter, it's human nature to believe what they hear. It helps that it's backed up with what they see: a successful couple comfortably ensconced in luxury.

A surprise guest brings up the rear: Ryan.

Whereas I'm slack-jawed, Jack smothers a snicker. "Look at him, the cock of the walk," he murmurs. "Wouldn't he have been less conspicuous as one of the help?"

"I'll let you broach that to him after tonight."

Jack shudders. "Heck, no! He'll have me on the very next Acme flight to Syria." Which is home to one of Acme's extraordinary rendition sites.

That doesn't stop me from taunting, *"bawk, bawk, chicken."*

"Senator Broderick Page and his wife, Jenny, are coming your way," Emma warns us.

Just as Broderick spots us, Jack leans in and kisses my cheek. I blush and honor him with an adoring gaze. When I look back in their direction, Broderick is staring at us. Catching my eye, he smirks, as if he caught us doing the dirty in the guest bathroom.

Watching him too, Jenny frowns, then follows his gaze to Jack and me.

Leaning into Jack, I whisper, "We're on our target's radar."

"The missus isn't pleased," he mutters.

"Something tells me she's used to it."

"You can use that to your advantage."

"I guess you can too." By my tone, he knows I don't look forward to either of our next moves: mine, to encourage Broderick; and his, to allow Jenny to cry on his shoulder.

While making his way over, Broderick glad-hands some of our other guests: politicians, lobbyists, donors. In the meantime, others come over to introduce themselves. One neighbor is a high-ranking cabinet member; Another is a Saudi banker. Both wangle for one-on-one time with "Aiden," who chuckles before informing them that when it comes to any business decisions we're joined at the hip. "Ruby is the gatekeeper," he explains. "All entreaties go through her."

Suddenly, they see me through new eyes.

Are those dollar signs twinkling in their corneas? So much for wanting to know the real me—

That is, the true Ruby.

May she rest in peace.

After they make their pitches—the cabinet member's is that the Spencers be her guests at a charity fundraiser; the banker's is an invitation to join him for tennis at D.C.'s most exclusive athletic club—I break the news that unfortunately, we're only in town for a few more days before jetting out again, but that I'll give them a call when we get back.

Now that the Pages are a few feet away, I turn to them. My smile is for Jenny, but when my eyes move to Broderick, he's primed to woo me. His wink makes this obvious. He's then got the nerve to pump Jack's hand as if they're long-lost brothers. His way of acknowledging me is a deferential nod followed by a reference to his days in "uni" in Edinburgh, with "H." By name-dropping Prince Harry, he's signaling his reputation as a scoundrel.

I purr, "You were mates, eh? That says a lot about you."

On Jody's cue, the orchestra plays a slow, sexy tune.

Broderick takes it upon himself to lead me onto the dance floor.

Jack is being more than a good sport to do the same with Jenny.

And so, it begins.

"OUR PATHS HAVE ALMOST CROSSED a few times," Broderick murmurs in my ear.

"Is that so?" I pull back so that he'll take note of my coyness. "I'm sure I'd remember."

"Davos. Two years ago. At least, it was rumored you were there."

"If I admit to it, will you keep it our little secret? Aiden pouts at the knowledge that anyone would know our whereabouts."

"How about you? Do you ever get tired of his game of hide and seek?"

I laugh. "I'm here, in your arms. Does that answer your question?"

"Someone had to ask you to dance."

"What do you mean by that?"

"Aiden was in no hurry"—Broderick pulls me closer—"to hold you in his arms."

"And you were?"

"You're here with me and not him, aren't you?"

"You're a guest. It would have been rude to say no."

"Admit it. You love it."

"You're right. Otherwise, the party falls short of all expectations."

He grins at my playful sarcasm. "I meant being in my arms," he insists.

"From where you've placed your hand, it doesn't seem your intentions are exactly honorable." By that, I mean it's on my bare back at the periphery of my hip.

He chuckles. "You're right. They aren't. Does that disappoint you?"

I shrug. "No. In fact, on the basest level, one could say it's flattering."

"Good, because you fascinate me." Broderick pulls me

even closer. "Despite your stiff-upper-lip routine, my guess is that you're somewhat intrigued by me too."

"Perhaps," I admit.

"Enough to chew through that leash Aiden has you tethered to?"

I gasp, then giggle. "It's not the leash but the jewel-studded collars that keep me at his side."

"Speaking of studs, I'll bet he's anything but. Admit it: he's deadly in the sack."

"Hardly." I nod over at Jenny. "I'll bet your wife could verify it."

She's dancing with Jack. Whether it's from tears or lust, her eyes are glassy. My guess is the former.

Par for the course when you're married to an obvious philanderer.

Broderick grins down at me. "Let me guess: Aiden is not above wife-swapping."

"I wouldn't know. He's never broached the topic." My eyes meet his. "How about you? Would it bother you if she went to bed with Aiden?"

It's Broderick's turn to shrug. "She's had worse."

"In other words, your trades are rarely fair."

He guffaws. "Powerful men rarely look like runway models, though I'm sure any gal would find Aiden easy on the eye." He pulls back to give me the once-over. "And rarely do powerful women look like you."

"Such flattery, Senator! It's all going to my head."

"You're being a cock tease." To prove it, he leans against me with his hardened member.

"Goodness! After such naughty talk, you deserve a bit of heartache... or some pain *somewhere*."

Realizing that the singer is on the last stanza, he leans in to close the deal: "I'll just bet you'd enjoy inflicting it on me. I know I would. Do you think you can get away?"

I shrug. "Aiden is meeting with our accountants tomorrow for a couple of hours. Perhaps you'd like to join me for tea."

"Here, you mean?"

"Tell him the St. Regis, penthouse suites," Emma whispers. "He's to ask for 'Mary Blythe.'"

"I'd prefer the St. Regis," I reply. "I keep a suite there, under the name of 'Mrs. Mary Blythe.' How about two o'clock?"

"I'll count down the minutes."

I can't get away from him quickly enough.

As I walk away, does he notice my shiver? Doubtful.

Jack uses my departure as an excuse to hand Jenny back to Broderick. She seems disappointed.

I can't say I blame her. It's disheartening to watch your husband openly woo other women, especially when his motive is yet another notch on his belt.

At least mine has the excuse that he's protecting our country.

***

An hour into the party, Kellie Diller, pretty in pink, makes her entrance. She's taller and even more stunningly beautiful than her photo.

Those who notice her freeze and stop mid-sentence if only for a moment: just time enough for their faces to register fear before they grit their teeth into steely smiles.

Their momentary silence has a ripple effect: everyone now knows she's arrived.

Kellie is an expert at reading a room. Noting that the other guests glance our way, she homes in on us too. Like a shark skimming through dark waters, her sultry stride parts the hushed crowd.

"Scary," Emma mutters.

Poor Jack.

His broad grin begs to differ, as does his open stance and outstretched hand.

But first, Abu insists that she go through the security protocol. She shrugs her annoyance but does so anyway. Abu empties her purse. Nothing. The same with her coat. Undeterred, he runs his security wand over her.

Again, nothing. Kellie bats her eyes at him. "Can I join the party now?"

Grudgingly, he waves her on.

She makes a beeline to "Aiden." When she reaches him, she pulls him close—too close, in my opinion. Her face, upturned, invites his lips to find hers.

Without hesitation, he accommodates.

Am I the only one who notices that she's placed her hand over his heart?

Where he's put his wrist is only seen by me: firmly on the curve of her ass.

I turn my head so that others miss my shock.

Not Broderick. In fact, he laughs.

What the hell just happened?

Broderick sidles over. "Tomorrow, when I'm done with you, you'll have forgotten all about his little indiscretion."

His declaration sounds more like a threat than a promise.

By MIDNIGHT, the last guests have taken their leave. Our team is exhausted.

I'm so much more than that. I am livid.

Despite this, I wait until Jody's crew has finished cleaning up and taken off and the others on our mission team have dispersed to their bedrooms—including Ryan, who raised a brow when I headed off to the master suite.

To hell with him. I'm due a well-earned night's sleep in the suite's most sumptuous boudoir.

Not Jack. He can bunk with Ryan for all I care.

To make that point, I lock the suite's door.

The suite has his-and-her bathrooms. I hear the shower running in his as I move to mine.

After releasing the sash that holds the halter of my dress to my neck, I pull it down over my hips, letting it drop to the floor. I resist the urge to toss it into the trash, but only because it's much too expensive. Instead, I'll give it to my favorite charity's consignment shop so that it brings some good into this dark, depraved world.

I'm washing my hair when I feel Jack's presence. "May I join you?"

"No."

That doesn't stop him from opening the glass door and entering.

He knows better than to touch me.

But I touch him. Make that *punch* him, in the gut.

When he rights himself, I slap his face.

Still, he keeps his hands to himself.

Until I cry. At that point he cradles my head to his chest.

I let him.

But that doesn't stop my sobbing.

Yes, he was doing his job. But why did he have to keep the where, when, and how from me? By doing so, he broke our recently agreed upon cardinal rule.

Reading my mind, he says, "As we discussed, I went with the others to hand-deliver the invitations. When Congress is in session, Kellie stays at a suite in the St. Regis. It was on my route. I wasn't expecting her to be there. When a servant answered, Kellie heard what I said to the woman and invited me in. Knowing that she'd also see me later this evening, I introduced myself."

"I'll just bet you did."

"It's the mission. She's the target." He strokes my arm. "We're also meeting privately tomorrow."

"Bullseye, Mr. Craig." My claps, slow and hard, propel droplets toward Jack's face.

His first instinct is to grab my hands.

His next is to pull me to him—

I meet his glare with mine.

He backs me against the shower's marble wall and raises one of my legs and wraps it high on his hip, grasping it so that I can't let go or else I'll slip and fall, taking him with me.

Instead, he takes me with him to the bed.

THE DISTANCE between anger and bliss is much more than eight stiff inches.

There are never enough huskily whispered I love you's to right the wrong of betrayal.

They say love means never having to say you're sorry. To hell with that! Every woman I know would beg to differ.

Tonight, I'd be the first to get in that line.

But that's just it: Jack wasn't betraying me. I'd been duly warned what this mission entailed.

And so had he.

By the time we exhaust our angst, envy, and lust, the sun is rising over the Washington Monument. Talk about a phallic symbol! It's an awful reminder of what awaits me in a mere eight hours.

Though I should be sleeping, instead I elect to make, and take, love. This activity is well worth it. Jack's desire girds me for the pain that comes with my pending personal disgust and humiliation, not to mention having to pretend otherwise.

As if reading my mind, Jack asks, "When do you meet with Broderick?"

"Two o'clock. At the St. Regis."

He frowns. "By then, I'll be with Kellie. Afterward, she's introducing me to those she calls 'the Inner Circle."

"With" is the operative word. "Afterward" is its confirmation. We both know it.

To get my mind out of his gutter, I ask, "Donors? Politicians? Russian operatives?"

"Those in the first two categories, for sure," he replies. "They'll join us later at her suite. From the adjacent one, Arnie and Abu will scan their devices for proof of treason."

I chuckle. "I'll bet Broderick is one of them.'

"I wouldn't doubt it." Jack strokes my arm. "Donna, seriously: this could be the whole ballgame."

"I hope you're right."

"Kellie is pulling out all stops to impress 'Aiden.' She's

bound and determined that he lays odds on her party, not Libby's."

"How do you know this? What exactly did she say?"

For one, and I quote, 'You took your time getting around to me.' And then, when she said goodbye, she added, "Now more than ever, I wish I was Ruby."

"What the hell do you think she meant by that?"

"I have no idea. It could just be her attempt at flirtatious wordplay before the Big Bang. I just did my best not to react. My guess: she was scolding 'Aiden' for not meeting her sooner."

"I'm sure you'll more than make it up to her." I look away. "I take it you weren't able to scan the mobile devices she keeps at home."

"Oddly enough, there was no mobile signal anywhere in her apartment."

"Don't you find that odd? I mean, nothing says 'I'm not in politics, instead I'm a Russian spy' than a dearth of mobile devices."

"All the more reason it's today's top priority." Jack grimaces. "Hopefully, Acme can finish the job once and for all—and net a few whoppers."

I snicker. "Yeah, well, fingers crossed. Hey, too bad you won't be with Jenny instead! All she wants is a shoulder to cry on."

"You kid, but I'm worried about her. She seems to be at her breaking point with Broderick." Jack clenches his fists. "If he offers her up to me again, I'll break his nose. And then I'll drive her to a battered woman's shelter. I don't want to be the one to push her over the edge."

Lucky Jenny! For once, she's not the sacrificial lamb.

Unlike me. Or, for that matter, Jack.

Reading my mood, Jack kisses my forehead. "What we do is the quickest way to infiltrate those who wish to bring our country to its knees. Or, in Kellie's words, 'Sex is the perfect form of terrorism. No bullets or bombs needed, just the erosion of our Constitution.'"

"Wow! How did that topic come up?"

He shrugs. "She works sex into every conversation."

I snort. "Talk about just putting it out there! As it pertains to the Constitution, she's wrong. There will be bullets and bombs. It's how they'll keep down those who stand up to them."

We hold each other tightly until the sun's rays have angled beyond the drapes and forces us to face today's missions.

Chapter 5

Presentiment

The feeling that something will, or is, about to happen is called a "presentiment."

Certainly, you've had one. For instance, when you didn't believe your husband when he told you he had to work late, you checked up on him. Yes, he was at work—but so was his assistant, and they were both naked.

In that case, your presentiment paid off.

You've got the hefty monthly alimony payments to prove it.

RIGHT ON TIME, Broderick knocks on the door of my hotel suite. I open it wearing a see-through negligee.

The senator walks in but leans against the door, closing it shut. With no hesitation, he takes me in his arms. When his mouth finds mine, he doesn't hesitate to pry it open.

I know I should lean into it, but after Jack's confession last night, I pull back.

Broderick does too. "I'm moving too fast, aren't I?" My pause is long enough that he frowns. "I just thought that... Well, last night you were ready, willing, and able."

What can I say to that? Certainly not the truth: that my change of heart is because I can't stomach him: a man who's a traitor.

And who, if Libby loses her re-election, will also be our country's next president.

He shrugs. "I... I won't force you. I respect that you don't want to betray your husband." Broderick bows his head.

Um...

Huh?

To show he means it, he drops to his knees at my feet and hugs my thighs under my negligee.

What the...

"—Especially now that I know Aiden created and finances Broken Wing." Broderick adds, "He and Kellie made the big announcement to our party's inner circle."

YES! The Spencers have warp-sped their way into it! *YES!*

Because I can't let on that I knew of my husband's whereabouts, I say, "Well, then, I'm glad he finally made the announcement. Because of our quest for privacy, we've stayed in the shadows. As you can imagine, supporting your organization is a very big decision for us."

Broderick nods. "From his jacket pocket, he pulls out a circular insignia ring and holds it up."Like Aiden and you, I don't wear it in public."

I take it in hand for a closer look. It's an eagle. One of its wings is broken.

"Great insignia, isn't it?" Broderick's eyes shine.

"Apropos," I concede.

"You're being too modest. Aiden told us you came up with the design, and the name of our private little club. Yep, Broken Wing is going to bring this country *to its knees!*" Broderick hoots as if we're at a football rally, and then rubs my rump.

What the...

Well, that certainly has my attention. I look down. Oddly, he's frowning. Okay, yeah, maybe I've put on a pound or two. But hey, it's all Grade A prime beef. Sharply, I ask, "What's the matter?"

"Nothing...It's just that..."

I must keep the upper hand. "Out with it." My tone is take-no-prisoners sharp.

Broderick's face is beet red. "It's just that I hadn't realized you've yet to be—well, you know—*initiated.*"

What the hell is he talking about?

In a sultry whisper, I coo, "Trust me: Aiden won't mind in the least if you, um, initiate me."

"Are you sure? I mean... I wouldn't want to do anything to make him upset."

Yikes I can't let him suspect I don't know what the heck he's talking about. "No issues. I mean that sincerely, Broderick. He won't be upset you did the honors. We're all on the same team, right?"

My declaration stirs him to smother me with kisses. When we part, he murmurs, "Then by all means, let's get on with it."

He moves behind me. Before I know it, he's placed both my hands on the buffet table. He lifts my negligee to my waist. "I promise to be gentle."

"I have no doubt." Can he tell my whisper is filled with resignation?

He loosens his tie then he drapes it over my mouth as a gag. "Close your eyes."

I brace myself...

Nothing.

I open my eyes. Through the mirror over the table, I notice he's taken off his ring. Not only that but he's holding it over the flame of his lighter.

Shite! He's going to *brand me?*

Gagged, my protests come out like sultry moans.

"Erotic, I know! As always, Aiden was right about the branding too. Not only is feeling the burn a turn-on but so is knowing we're all part of one great oneness, all the while hiding it from the very people we're out to destroy! It's, like, *orgasmic!*" He looks down at his pants tent. "Jeez, I get a woody just thinking about it!" He pats my ass. "Ruby, I was honored to have been at his—and *your*—coming out party last night. And now, to have his approval to initiate you into our cause... I can't describe the high!"

If he thinks he's high now, I wonder how he'll feel when I shove him out the window?

Why the hell didn't Jack warn me?

Maybe it's best that he didn't.

Holding as tight as I can to the buffet, I growl, "Let's get this over with."

Not that Broderick can make out my words.

There will be payback—

Not just for him, but for Jack too.

———

THE GUTTURAL CURSES I release when the gag comes off are reason enough for Broderick to leave immediately. He's right. There would be little mitigation in shooting the messenger.

But one doesn't know until one tries. Maybe it's a good thing he elected not to test the theory.

Even for the several blocks between the St. Regis and the Watergate, sitting in a cab ride would have been agonizing. Instead, I walk back, taking a circuitous route suggested to me by Emma, who still has eyes and ears on me.

When I apologized for screaming so loud when he branded me," she muttered, "Better you than me."

A couple of hours later, Jack is back from his rendezvous with Kellie. Having heard my groans, his knock is gentle. "May I enter?"

He does so anyway and finds me sitting in a tub of warm water and Epson salts. He recoils at my glare.

"You could have warned me!" I declare.

"About what?"

"What do you think? *ABOUT THE BRANDING!*" I toss a bar of soap at him.

His jaw drops. "I did, Donna! I swear!"

"Not in a timely fashion. But I get it. You were too busy keeping Kellie occupied." I turn away from him. "Imagine Broderick's surprise that I didn't have the ring, not to mention the tattoo! So, to prove my loyalty to Broken Wing's cause, I insisted that he do the honor of initiating me. The last thing I assumed was that it meant being branded by his ring!" I shake away the frustration of my blithe stupidity.

Noting that my scowl isn't going anywhere, Jack explains: "Apparently, the real Aiden came up with the bright idea of identifying his cabal's members by giving them a ring. He also insisted that they be branded with its insignia."

"Is Broken Wing aligned with Russia? Or is it just another version of a Trillionaire Boy's Club that wants to control all politicians up for dibs?"

Jack frowns. "Good question. My guess: the answer is buried deep in Aiden's server farms."

"So tell me: how did you explain away the fact that you didn't have either the ring or the tattoo?" I ask.

"I didn't have to. Before our party, Abu secured the suite beside hers in the St. Regis so that we can conduct reconnaissance. This morning, while she was at her party's headquarters, Abu and Arnie went in and planted security cameras. When she came back, she took a shower. ComInt noticed the tattoo, and that the same insignia was on her ring. It correctly deduced it was how Broken Wing members identified themselves to others in the cabal. But by the time Abu and Arnie could secure a facsimile of the ring and a stick-on tattoo, I was already in her suite. Abu slipped it to me when he knocked on her door with a complimentary bucket of champagne."

"Well, well! Lucky you! More bedtime stories to be recorded, I'm sure."

Jack ignores my sarcasm. "I texted you immediately to check our Watergate mailbox for your ring and tattoo."

I shake my head. "Nope, I never received any message, from you or from Emma."

"Emma, is that true?" Jack asks.

"Affirmative. And since I'm copied on all mission communications, I didn't get it, either," she announces. "Arnie has mentioned that Aiden and Ruby's apartment is a cell service dead zone. This proves him right. He's been trying to track down the apartment's mobile blockers so he can modify their settings to read Acme's only. Over and out."

That's Emma's way of giving us some sorely needed space.

"I'm sorry, Donna, for your unnecessary pain." Jack sits on the side of the tub.

My anger has subsided enough that I now shrug away his apology. "By the way, Broderick also said that 'Aiden' had told him 'Ruby' came up with the name."

"Weird, since I never told him anything of the sort." Jack shakes his head, stymied.

"Maybe it was something the real Aiden said to him prior to the crash," I reply.

"Impossible. Before we played the Spencers, no one ever met them in person," he reminds me. "Perhaps via text before the crash."

"Maybe," I concede. "In any regard, Kellie and her cohorts can kiss your ring for real!"

"Believe me, they did." He shudders. "Hey, whenever you're ready, we'll check the box together."

"We won't need the tattoo sticker, now that I have the real deal."

Jack winces at my sarcasm. "Listen, Don, the sooner we

pull together a full list of Broken Wing members, the quicker this mission ends, and the sooner we can go home."

The thought of Kellie laughing at my comeuppance is enough for me to slip under the water's surface.

I'm six minutes under when Jack pulls me out. He knows I could have stayed that way for another minute. That said, I'm glad he's concerned enough to stop me from testing my lung capacity.

It's best that I save my energy for the next unpleasant surprise.

To our relief, the mailroom is empty.

Jack is just about to use our key to open the box when the door opens. To give us cover, he leans into me. When his lips meet mine, I melt into his kiss. It's all for show.

Okay, not really.

Usually, such intimate moments have the desired effect: the interloper is embarrassed enough to retreat. Instead, we hear a chuckle. "*Donna... and Jack?* Wow! Fancy meeting you here!"

Astounded, we turn toward the very recognizable voice. We aren't mistaken. It's Carol Wise. This very dear friend of Ryan's is also the executive director of the NSA's National Counterterrorism Center.

She wears running shoes, shorts, and an oversized tee-shirt. Her hair is pulled back in a high ponytail. Sweat glistens on her exposed arms. Instinctively, I go in for a hug, but she takes a step back. "As sticky as I am, trust me, I'm doing you a favor."

I laugh but peck her cheek anyway. "You're worth it."

Noting that we stay put, her eyes go wide. "If I'm interrupting something..."

Jack's chagrin mirrors mine.

"Got it." Carol reaches toward the mailbox—

But instead, she opens the one beside it. Glancing up, she can't help but notice that Jack's gaze moves from her box —2722—to the Spencers' at 2720.

"I take it you've got my next-door neighbors, the Spencers, under surveillance?"

"You could say that." I show her the mailbox key. "Have you met them?"

"Never! Neither here in the mailroom, or for that matter, anywhere else in the Watergate. Not even in the hall, though we're next-door neighbors."

"Oh...So... You know they recently had a party?" Jack asks.

Carol's cheeks pink up. "Yes... But... I wasn't invited. Not that I'd have expected an RSVP."

Noting my embarrassment, she adds, "I take it you somehow attended?"

The question is innocent enough. The fact that she even asked proves that Ryan hasn't clued her in on the mission per DNI Branham's directive.

Carol chuckles. "Since I imagine all answers are on a need-to-know basis, let's pretend I didn't ask." Her way of letting us off the hook is to open her mailbox. It's got a few envelopes that could pass as bills. But there is also a pale blue greeting card. She's curious enough to check out the sender's name, blushes, then slips it into the middle of the rest of her mail. Nodding, she says. "It's great seeing you, Craigs." After a pause, she then adds, "Look, I have two mailbox keys. Take this one...just in case."

"But... Why?" I ask.

"In case you ever need to get a message to...well, to the rest of your team..." She shrugs. "It may sound odd but something our mailman once said about the Spencers makes me think that nothing about them is what it seems—including their mailbox."

I want to laugh because Carol doesn't know how right she is! If only Ryan could read her into this mission—

But that would put her life in danger. It's the last thing he'd want to do.

That shouldn't stop us from taking her up on her offer. In fact, my guess is that Ryan would hope that we did. "Thanks, Carol." I take the key. "You're right. It may come in handy.

"By the way, what exactly did the mailman say?" Jack asks.

"That the Spencers never get any mail. None at all! Odd, isn't it? Or perhaps not. They may have consolidated its delivery to one of their other homes." Carol shrugs. "Give my best to Ryan." She leaves, closing the door behind her.

After pocketing her key, I unlock the Spencers' box. The only thing inside is a tiny envelope. I open it. As Jack insisted, it holds the sticker that would have saved me from being branded. The ring is also enclosed.

"Arnie, why wasn't I informed that my sticker was in the Spencers' box?" I ask.

No answer.

"Arnie, please respond!" Jack demands.

Still nothing.

"He's been incommunicado for at least four minutes.

Just a few seconds ago, I lost the video feed for the server room!" Emma doesn't sound happy. "He warned me this could happen, especially if it got too hot for the video feed. The last thing I heard was him shouting—really, cursing about something! It sounded as if he said he'd gotten burned!" We hear Emma's frantic keyboard clicks.

"We're headed there now," Jack vows.

Supposedly, the Spencers' private elevator moves at WARP speed. It doesn't seem that way when a life may be in danger.

The server room is hot enough to be a desert. No wonder the computers seem to be screaming. A few are on fire. There is no movement of air; in fact, there's no air at all.

Arnie is passed out on the floor. His arms and hands are scorched.

Despite this, Jack grabs him under his arms and drags him out the door, I run to the thermostat. By now, I'm gasping for oxygen. But no matter how hard I try to tap in the coolest setting, it won't budge.

There's only one thing left for me to do:

Using my diamond ring, I scratch a large circle on the glass—

Then I shoot at it.

As the circle shatters, cool air flows in through the hole.

By now Abu, Ryan, and Dominic are also here.

Just in time, too, because I'm dizzy...

And I faint...

Chapter 6

Intentionality and Intensity

*D*o you have what it takes to survive an apocalypse?

In this environment, survival depends on intentionality and intensity. Any aspect of human culture that people assume gets transmitted automatically without too much conscious deliberation goes by the slang word "NGMI " and means "not going to make it." Languages will disappear, churches will be a thing of the past, political ideals will die, art will go underground, and the capacity to read and write and figure mathematically won't be taught.

In time, the reproduction of our species will fail —

Except among people who are deliberate and self-conscious and a little bit fanatical about ensuring that the things they love are carried forward.

Is that you? Do you have the tenacity? Can you stay the course?

YES! You've got this thing!

Just think of it as a run in your pantyhose. It's beside the

*point that you no longer wear any. And you certainly won't
be wearing them during the End of Days.*

That's okay. Camo suits you much better.

I WAKE up in my bed. My mission team is gathered around
me, including Ryan. When I try to sit up, Jack eases me
down. "Keep still, Don, and take slow, deep breaths."

I nod and accommodate.

"I know you're worried about Arnie," Jack continues.
"So, before you ask, the answer is yes: he's doing okay. But
because his arms are badly burned, Acme's doctors insist on
a head-to-toe check-up. He'll be out of commission for at
least a week. By then, he may not be incapacitated by his
wounds. If not, he'll be cleared for duty."

Relieved, I nod again.

Ryan looks over at Abu. "I guess that means it's up to
you to disengage the Spencers' Palm Beach server farm," he
says.

"Yes, sir." The seriousness of Abu's response shows his
concern for our colleague. Like the rest of us, he won't let
Arnie down.

"Donna, Acme's med techs are on their way to give you
the all-clear. When they do, Jody would like to dress you."
Ryan informs me. "Her team is coordinating tonight's event
that introduces the Spencers to Libby's big-ticket donors.
Thankfully, POTUS is out stumping in the Midwest, so she
can't blow our covers. For this shindig, Lee will be the big
draw."

After kissing me gently on the forehead, Jack stands up.

"Then we better let the med techs do their jobs. In fact, I've got to take off for my next appointment."

"Where to?" I ask.

"Congresswoman Calloway has asked to meet me prior to the event"—grimacing, he adds—"in private."

"In private" says it all. I close my eyes and tilt my face downward so that no one can see my dismay.

"Then you'd better get going, since both you and your target will want to have plenty of time to clean up before Libby's grand entrance," Ryan replies.

Jack and Gabriella may be doing the deed, but no one will feel dirtier than me.

Despite this, my husband kisses my forehead and heads out.

Noting my scowl, Ryan covers my hand with his. "He's only doing his job."

"Yes—and he does it *so well*."

Ryan winces at my sarcasm. "Speaking of honeytraps, Senator Lassiter will also be attending. Are you, er, up for the task?"

"Aye, aye, sir. Unless the med tech says otherwise." *Please let that be the case...*

"I'll send him right in." Ryan rises. "The sooner we have proof on Lassiter and Calloway, the sooner you and Jack can go home."

"I'll drink to that—later, at tonight's shindig."

I don't like Ryan's frown.

I look him in the eye. "Is there something you're not telling me, boss?"

"I should warn you. Lassiter isn't exactly known for his erotic prowess."

"You're saying that I may get a reprieve? In my book, that's a good thing!"

Ryan leans in. "Let me put it this way: if he gives you an out, it may not be the lesser of two evils."

I guffaw. "That's easy for you to say. Try walking a block in my stilettos."

In all the years we've known each other, I've never seen Ryan blush as deeply as he does now. And yet, for some reason, he doesn't feel the need to be more specific.

Frankly, I'm fine with that.

Jody's med tech taps on the door, giving Ryan the out he needs.

I wish I could say the same, but, drat, the med tech gives me a clean bill of health.

Since Abu is disabling the server farm, Ryan is helping Dominic to collect all mobile devices from our party guests. Our boss now sports a wig, glasses, and a mustache. I can't laugh or he'll glower at me.

Once again, Jody has outdone herself in creating a fairytale environment for the Spencers' guests. This time, it's a quintet playing classical music, low lighting that twinkles from on high, and delicacies either passed on trays or carved at the stations strategically placed throughout the room.

The same goes for tonight's dress: a fifteen-thousand-dollar Oscar de la Renta ombré sequined fringe column gown with a silk crew neck and sleeveless. By the time its top-to-bottom body-hugging bodice reaches its fringe skirt, its color palette morphs from silver to gold to bronze, which is also the color of my heels.

Having seen a picture of Wilbur Lassiter, I spot him easily in the thick crowd. Jack has yet to appear. Neither has Gabriella. I guess their liaison went as well as Acme had hoped.

Wilbur joins the line to greet me. A few moments before he reaches my side, I feel an arm go around my waist. Jack smiles. "Sorry I'm late."

"As long as you were successful."

"Yeah...about that..."

Before he can say another word, I sing out, "Senator Lassiter! How nice of you to join us."

I've just killed two birds with one stone. Now Jack's recitation of the latest notch on his belt won't turn me into the party's Debbie Downer. It also warns him that everything he does and says can be used against him by this little old man who just so happens to head up the Judiciary, Foreign Relations, and Homeland Security & Government Affairs committees: the first, very publicly, and the other committees with whatever blackmail he holds over his party colleagues who chair them. Despite being the spitting image of the Monopoly Man, these are the real reasons he's known by that nickname in Foggy Bottom's hallowed halls.

He takes my extended hand and kisses it, murmuring "*Enchanté*" in his renowned Foghorn Leghorn drawl. "This day is one I've looked forward to for many a year!"

"We're flattered," I reply. "And honored that you accepted our invitation."

"I'd be a fool not to," he declares. Leaning into me, he murmurs, "And you were very smart to extend it—*finally.*"

With a mirthless chuckle, he adds, "I was beginning to think you and your mister were ghosts."

"You're right, we were remiss not to do so earlier." Jack holds out his hand. "I got the same lecture just this afternoon from Gabriella."

"So she mentioned." Wilbur's smile is too broad, too white, and too even to be nature's gift. I wonder if it keeps his sunken eyes and thin-skinned visage from scaring the wee ones on Halloween night. I'd imagine any Congressperson coming upon him in a dark Georgetown alley before sunrise might yelp and then pledge to vote any way he requests.

He nods in my direction. "I'll let your pretty li'l missus make it up to me."

Lucky me. I swear, this mission gets worse with each passing minute.

"Sure, name it," Jack replies.

I resist the urge to kick him in the shin.

"Gabriella mentioned that Ruby and you are hunters. In my book, a woman who doesn't faint at the sight of Bambi's blood and isn't afraid she'll break a nail while holding a rifle is worth her weight in gold. It would be my honor to host you at my li'l ranch. It's just an hour away, in Virginia. It's got a rifle range, and I've stocked my woods with all kinds of tasty critters. Perhaps we'll track down a few." Licking his thin lips, he adds, "There's no better meal than one you've killed yourself."

"Sounds like fun," I purr. "A family estate, is it?"

"Hardly. I grew up hardscrabble. But I learned quickly that being elected to public office has its benefits, especially when it comes to real estate. But don't expect too much.

Udder Delights is just an itty-bitty cabin on a few acres of woods."

"You call it 'Udder Delights?' My, my! What a pithy play on words," I murmur. "By its name, I take it you also raise cattle?"

"Hell, no! Can't stand the smell of cow crap!" Wilbur rolls his eyes. "It's called that because I've staffed it with some big-breasted gals. Most of them formerly worked at a restaurant that hired them solely for the size of their best assets. My male guests enjoy a little eye candy—especially when my buxom baby girls are willing to clean their guns too, if you get my drift. Better to sample the bonbons in the privacy of your home is my motto. Am I right?" He pokes Jack with his elbow. "Makes it harder for the more skittish gals to prove anything in court—especially after they've signed an NDA."

I murmur, "Do tell." *Not.*

"You're in for a treat too, Ruby. Udder Delights is stocked with some man meat; you know, the kind you find at those bars where women go to ogle male dancers who wear them tiny jock straps."

I raise a brow. "You've thought of everything."

"Indeed, I have!" He chuckles. "Ah, but I'd only be preaching to the choir, now, wouldn't I, Mrs. Spencer? You of all people know that quid pro quo makes the world go 'round. For my Udder Delights guys and gals, the pay is much better than what they were getting in those strip joints: just minimum wage. So are the tips." Wilbur elbows Jack. "If not mine, at least those of my well-endowed colleagues."

Jack's reaction: he chokes on his gin and tonic. Better

that than a tech bro-worthy high-five, which might have knocked Wilbur on his ass.

Then again, maybe that wouldn't have been so bad.

"How positively quaint." My sarcasm is not lost on Wilbur, who chortles gleefully.

"I guarantee you; Udder Delights is anything but. I aim to please my guests."

"Looking forward to it." I coo.

That earns me a pinch to my cheek: the one on my face, though he's not opposed to taking a quick glance at the ones on my backside.

Wilbur's face is wrinkled enough that I stifle a shudder at the thought that I'll have to validate if his ass is just as prune pocked. If so, it may be too distorted for me to tell if it sports the Broken Wing brand. On the other hand, if I find a suspicious-looking mole, I'll suggest he have his doctor look at it. Or not.

Wilbur winks at Jack. "I hope you'll join us, too."

Jack shakes his head. "Wish I could, but Gabriella insists I make the rounds on Capitol Hill. There are a few of your party members she'd like to introduce me to. And since POTUS's campaign manager, Tommy Jensen, will be joining us, I can't very well say no."

"Aw, shucks. You'll be sorely missed." Wilbur's smirk doesn't tamp down his glee at my bad luck.

Jack ignores my glare for good reason: the quintet is playing *Hail to the Chief*.

Libby... *is here?*

Jack looks just as surprised as me.

So does Ryan, who's smart enough to duck behind a column before her Secret Service detail spots him.

Libby's Chief of Staff, Tommy Jensen, is at her side. One of his hands—I assume it's the frostbitten one—is gloved. The other points at us. When he sees he's got my attention, he waves timidly.

There's nothing I can do but wave back—

And then I realize there are two others in their party: Lee and Eve. When our eyes meet, Lee laughs so hard that he doubles over.

As I shake my head, he places a finger to his lips.

Even knowing our secret is safe with him, will Libby recognize us?

We'll know soon because they're headed our way.

———

LIBBY'S PATH meanders to accommodate fawning tributes from the Spencers' awed party guests. Every couple of yards she is stopped by an adoring lobbyist, politician, or big-buck donor. She's gracious enough to shake a hand, share a giggle, or lean intently toward those who think she's got their full attention, if only for a few seconds.

All the while, Jack mutters a few choice oaths, cursing our bad luck at Libby's awful timing.

I'm sure that Lee's unexpected appearance has something to do with it too.

By now, Wilbur has made his way to Libby's side. He plays the role of adoring vassal-slash-fawning sycophant to the hilt. Surely, Libby realizes he's the first in her party who would stick a knife in her back! Not that I can tell her—

Until we have the proof.

And maybe not even then. If in fact he's the saboteur, Acme's mandate is a quieter exit strategy for the perp.

A shame. Anyone who's out to kill POTUS deserves a firing squad. Of course, one well-placed bullet in her adversary's heart (head, neck, you name it) accomplishes the same goal.

Better Wilbur than Bambi.

By now, Libby is just twenty feet away. Tommy leans over to whisper something in her ear. Her head turns to Jack and me.

She scowls.

Aw, hell, we're busted.

Libby is enough of a politician to grace us with a grand smile and walk over. Holding out her hand, she says, "I've been looking forward to finally meeting you, Mrs. and Mr. Spencer."

"The honor is all ours." How I'm able to squeak that out —in a British accent, no less—is truly a miracle.

Lee covers his snicker with a cough.

Eve is concerned enough to pat his back. Well, at least I have her fooled, if no one else.

Porter stares at me too, but his furrowed brow is evidence that he hasn't yet placed me. When he does, he'll want us to explain ourselves. Will he be satisfied with a warning that it's above his pay grade? Only if it comes from Lee.

Craving a sliver of Libby's spotlight, Gabriella and Wilbur hover within feet of her. Porter, realizing this too, touches his nose. From Lee's slight nod, I take it as a shorthand signal from their security playbook. Shaking Jack's hand, he declares, "Mr. Spencer, so great to finally meet you —and you as well, Mrs. Spencer."

"Likewise," says Jack.

"Our pleasure indeed," I add.

"Perhaps there is a place where Madam President and I can speak to you alone?" Lee suggests.

Jack nods. "This way, please." Taking my hand, Jack leads Libby's entourage to the library.

When Tommy, Gabriella, and Wilbur fall in line, Porter raises a brow at the head agent on Libby's Secret Service team, Betsy Proctor. Following his lead, Betsy blocks Libby's campaign manager, the congresswoman, and the senator from following us.

I can't resist the urge to glance back. As I'd imagined, Gabriella is seething. Wilbur knows better than to raise his voice above a hiss, but I can make out a few phrases: "How dare you!..." for one; and "You don't know who you're dealin' with, sir! I'll see that you're working the graveyard shift at Arlington Cemetery!..." for another.

Too bad. My money is on Porter.

Eve's attempt to calm him down is to rave about hearing "your wonderful ranch, Udder Delights, made last month's cover of *Architectural Digest!* How prestigious!"

Playing to his ego seems to work. Once again, he's all moonlight-and-magnolias charming.

If I hear any more, I may barf. I take the lesser of the two evils facing me and follow the others behind closed doors.

Chapter 7

Fallout Shelter

*I*n *1959, the U.S. Government's Office of Civil and Defense Mobilization published and widely distributed a pamphlet entitled* The Family Fallout Shelter. *Within its spare thirty-two pages, illustrations of how to build shelters are interspersed with how the government envisioned life would carry on in these underground bunkers for weeks on end.*

Never mind that radioactive fall-out would affect Mother Earth for decades if not centuries.

One estimate puts the number of shelters built at 200,000, even though, by 1961, 53 percent of the population believed nuclear war was imminent.

So, who were really the proverbial ostriches with their head in the sand: those who built the shelters, or those who didn't?

Does it really matter? I mean, all's well that ends well.

For now, anyway.

THE LEADERS of Libby and Lee's security teams go into the library with us, but three agents are left outside the closed door. Jack and I motion Libby, Lee, and Eve to sit, but we say nothing until we gauge how angry POTUS is at our deception.

Libby has taken one of the room's two upholstered chairs. Her stare is laser sharp. Lee's chair faces hers. Far from being uncomfortable, he's yet to lose his bemused smirk.

Jack and I sit on the divan between them. Knowing my husband, we're thinking the same thing: *Ryan is going to be upset that we've blown the mission in the worst possible way.*

"Mr. and Mrs. Spencer, I realize that, during an election year, every politician has come hat in hand to you. In that way, I am no different."

What the...

She still thinks we're the Spencers?...

Well, I'll be damned.

"If my track record is any proof, you know that I've always put the good of our country before anything else," Libby continues. "I've assured, and delivered, the strongest military in our lifetime. I've got the support of the European Union. We've stabilized relations with China and have achieved economic parity. It's now our third biggest trading partner behind our bordering neighbors, Canada and Mexico..."

Suddenly she stops to rub her left eye. "Darn it!" she mutters. "Now the contact has rolled out of my other eye, too!" She stands up. "I must apologize. I keep these things in long enough that they dry out! But it has never happened in the middle of my dog-and-pony show."

"Tut, tut! We mustn't have that!" I sigh grandly. "Thank goodness America's Fourth Estate doesn't know what it should do about us. If we were in my birth country, tomorrow's *Daily Mail* headline would read, 'Which Spencer made POTUS cry?'"

Everyone laughs.

"There's a bathroom further down the hall, if you wish to take them out," Jack assures her.

Libby nods gratefully. "Lee, while the pony in our act takes care of her eyes, you don't mind being the dog and taking over, do you?" Libby pumps my hand, then heads out the door.

Betsy is right on her heels.

Lee looks from Jack, and then to me. "Let's hear it, Craigs. I'm sure it's a doozy."

Jack starts: "Listen...We can't! It's—"

"Let me make this easy for you. Upon hearing that Libby was headed your way, DNI Branham read me in on your mission."

Jack sighs. "Well...that's a relief."

"That's easy for you to say," Lee retorts.

"I take it he didn't exactly spell it out," I reply.

"Let's just say Marcus couldn't have been more cryptic. Or, as he put it: 'Acme has eyes and ears on the Spencers. It's a Ghost Protocol procedure, and it should stay that way at all costs.'"

I must know: "Would you have known us otherwise?"

Lee rolls his eyes. "You're actually asking me that?"

I feel my face heating up. No better time to change the

subject: "We've made contacts with two possible espionage suspects here at the party. A third is yet to be interrogated. Since this person is likely to hit the road later tonight, either Jack or I must intercept him before he leaves the party."

"Then I'll leave you to it." Lee stands up.

He's heading for the door when Jack declares, "Donna, I've got Jensen. Instead, go ahead and finalize your plans with Senator Lassiter."

Frowning, Lee stares at Jack. "By that, I take it you're allowing that little creep to sexually abuse *her*? How could you?"

"He's under suspicion for the recent attack on POTUS," Jack argues. "If so, she'll do what's necessary to uncover his role in facilitating it, and to learn what else he and his associates have planned. It's what she does—what we both do. Or have you forgotten that?"

"I wish I could." Lee mutters.

"If I can live with it, so can you." The heartache in my husband's voice brings tears to my eyes.

Lee stops cold. "You're a fool to keep telling yourself that." His gaze moves to me. "And so are you."

Watching Jack's hands tighten into fists is all it takes for Porter to hustle Lee out the door. It slams behind them.

I walk over to Jack and put my hand over his heart. I thought this would calm him down. But when he shoves it away, I realize I'm sorely mistaken.

"Despite claiming to be in love with Eve—not to mention hearing you tell him point blank that under no circumstances will you ever return his undying affection, that jerk has yet to get over you!"

"That's on him, so please don't take it out on me," I retort.

"You're right. I shouldn't." Jack admits. "And perhaps I wouldn't lose my cool if he didn't make it so damn obvious every time he's in the same room with you. Right now, the last thing we need is the added pressure of him fawning over you."

"I think he got the message loud and clear."

"Yeah, okay...we'll see about that." Jack looks down at the Patek Phillippe on his wrist. Despite wearing everything well, he's no clothes horse. Nor is he impressed by labels. When I asked Jody how she got him to wear it, she giggled. "I told him it was a knock-off."

"Well, then you better hope he doesn't break it or lose it."

"That's okay. I'll just take the deed to your house to even the score."

If that isn't incentive enough for me to hand the watch back to her the second the party is over, I don't know what is.

Jack nods toward the door. "We better get out there with the rest of our guests. While you keep Lassiter engaged, I'll put Tommy to the test."

"Got it." We walk out hand in hand.

JACK IS JUST as disappointed as me to see Wilbur talking to Lee. Still, he nudges me in their direction before heading toward Tommy, who stands with Gabriella and Libby in the middle of a group of high-rolling donors.

By the way Libby is squinting, I take it she still can't see out of one eye. Frankly, I'm relieved.

Seeing me approach, Wilbur announces, "Well, speak of the devil!" In a moment, he's at my side. The next thing I know, he's steering me toward Lee. "Mrs. Spencer, it turns out that our vice-presidential candidate is also a gun enthusiast. I've invited him to join us tomorrow at Udder Delights. I hope you don't mind."

"*Mr. Chiffray?*... Oh!... Not at all." I shrug so that neither man can gauge my relief.

"Blair House is just a couple of miles from the Watergate. My entourage will pick you up and we'll ride over together," Lee suggests.

Wilbur hides his disappointment well.

Too bad. If need be, I'll stick at Lee's side like glue.

It sure beats whatever Wilbur has planned for me.

Chapter 8

Eschatology

The part of theology that studies the End of Days is known as "eschatology."

It is derived from the ancient Greek word "ἔσχᾰτος" (pronounced "éskhatos") and literally means "end."

And not in a good way.

To be specific, it is an adjective used by several religions when describing the death of humanity as world events reach their final climax.

Folks: let's not mince words. If you combine the words "last" and "worst," you'll get the full gist of what it means.

Which brings us to a reality check: You don't have a basement big enough to store all the bottled water you'd need to wait out the return of Life As We Know It.

In other words, if the fallout doesn't kill you, the plastic particles in your drinking water will.

Suggestion: find a well-stocked wine cellar and hunker down for the long haul.

I meet Lee's motorcade inside the Watergate's secure underground parking lot. To my surprise, Eve is not with him.

"Where's your better half?" I ask.

"Libby's campaign aides have filled her weekend with public appearances," Lee explains. "All great stuff and right up her alley: hospitals, schools, and homeless shelters."

"You two make a great team," I reply.

"Yeah... I guess we do." Lee's tone says it all: *I wish she were you.*

Too bad. Ain't happening.

"Where's Jack?" he asks.

"With Gabriella. He's vetting her. She's on our suspect list."

"'Vetting,' eh? I guess that's as good a nickname for it as any."

"While he's at it, he'll vet Tommy Jensen too."

"Not in the same manner, I suppose." He purses his lips to hide his grin.

I warn, "Don't be cute."

"You're right. That's hitting below the belt." He laughs.

"What say we stay away from any discussion of nether regions for the rest of the weekend?" I suggest. "Wilbur makes too many innuendoes as is. I don't need them from you too."

"You're right. You don't." And now that we've set a few ground rules, it's a perfect time to bring up something I hope will put a smile on Lee's face: "How are Janie and Harrison taking the news about your run for office?"

"It's just as you'd imagine. Janie has had her fill of the limelight. She wants to be a normal Hilldale teen, not scrutinized for every little movement," Lee admits. "Being wealthier than many of the kids in school already puts her in an awkward position."

"And now that you're Libby's running mate, it's even more so."

He forces a grin. "Go to the head of the class, Mrs. Craig."

"Trisha will always be there for her," I remind him.

"From the looks of things, so will Jeff." This time, his smile is genuine. "He's a lot like his dad, you know; true blue, great sense of humor, good looking... and a one-man woman."

"You forget, Lee. Jeff's father—and for that matter, Mary's and Trisha's too—was Carl. He was an assassin, a terrorist, a blatant womanizer, and let's not forget he was also a blackmailer—yours, when you were in the White House."

"Then maybe it's a good thing your children never really knew their birth father. As far as they're concerned, Jack raised them to be the people they are now." Lee sighs. "Which is why I'll never understand how he can let you do... well, *this*." He stares out the window.

I have no answer to that. We both know Jack hates this part of our jobs.

I do too.

The rest of the ride is made in silence.

It's for the best.

Despite what Wilbur said, his estate is not some "itty-bitty cabin." Its nine-foot stone wall runs for miles alongside the property, which entails rolling hills and deep pine forests.

There are guards at its gate who explain that the "cabin" is another four miles up the winding driveway. When it comes into view, it's humongous: not a hotel, but the antithesis of Wilbur's description.

Lee echoes my observation with a drawn-out whistle. "Lassiter considers this 'itty-bitty'? It's larger than the Taj Mahal!"

I snort. "He has the gift of understatement."

"Nah, he loves to mislead," Lee retorts. "I wonder what other surprises he has in store for us?"

"Be careful what you wish for." My warning is as much for me as it is for Lee.

When our limo reaches the massive front steps, two attendants step forward to open the doors. Both are in their early twenties, one of each gender. They wear athletic togs that cling to their best assets: for the man, it's his broad shoulders, slim waist, and athlete's physique. The woman's tiny waist is offset by large high breasts. Her tennis skirt is short enough that when she bends down to pick up one of Lee's overnight bags, her thong is exposed. There's a butterfly tattoo on the back of her thigh.

Having just opened the door, the man has caught Lee's shock and awe. "That's Taffy," he divulges. "She'll be your personal concierge, Lee." His eyes meet mine. "And I'm Ken. I'll be yours, Ruby."

I hold out my hand so that he can help me out of the car. In Ruby's voice, I reply ever so sweetly, "Nice to meet you,

Ken. You may call me Mrs. Spencer. And this is Mr. Chiffray."

Ken's face turns red. He gets the message: friendly, but not familiar.

He's not angry. He's scared.

Interesting.

The round foyer has five halls. Ken takes the one in the middle. His walk is more of a strut, as if he knows I'm watching.

That's just it: he *hopes* that's the case.

Why is he trying so hard?

Taffy is doing the same for Lee: walking just a few steps ahead, sashaying her hips.

Ken stops at a room, takes out the key, and opens it.

Taffy stops at a door much further down but next to mine.

I enter a large, plush suite. It is round and has windows on three sides. The bed, a round California king, is dead-center and faces the windows. It looks out onto an expansive field.

"Beautiful, isn't it?" Ken lifts my suitcase onto a table. "Should I unpack for you?"

"No. You may leave."

"Oh...kay." He frowns. "But just so you know, I'm at your beck and call."

"Brilliant." I'm being sarcastic.

Not to be deterred, he walks over to a small chest. Turns out it's a bar. "Maybe you'd like some champagne." When Ken turns around, he has an iced bucket holding a bottle in one hand and two flutes in another.

"No thank you. You're dismissed."

Suddenly Ken is on his knees in front of me. "I'm here to give you anything you want." To make his point, he strokes my thigh.

To make mine, I raise my knee fast and high. When it hits his chin, his head snaps back. Reeling away, he lets loose with a pained gurgle before landing on his ass. He curls into a fetal position.

Since I've made my point, I wait silently for him to crawl out. Instead, he mutters, "If I... If I fail at ... at seducing you, I'm... a dead man."

I lean close and whisper, "Save yourself, Ken. Get away from here."

He's crying harder now and still gasping for air. In time, he's able to say: "It's too late for that."

"It's never too late." I walk over to the desk. From a memo pad adorned with the cabin's insignia, I rip off a page. "Hand this to one of Mr. Chiffray's Secret Service agents. They'll keep you safe until we leave."

Nodding, he takes it and runs out.

Did Taffy pull the same stunt with Lee? My guess is yes.

For the first time, I notice that the wall between his suite and mine share a door. I walk over and turn the knob.

I'm not surprised that it's unlocked. Possibly it's another of Wilbur's little games. I open it anyway.

Lee sits in an armchair by the room's fireplace. At first, he's startled to have been caught off-guard. But then realizing I'm the intruder, he beckons me over. "My Secret Service detail's audio feeds are cutting in and out."

At that point, I realize I haven't heard Emma's voice in my ear for quite some time. I whisper: "Acme ComInt, please respond."

Crickets.

"Emma?"

Nothing.

I shift my gaze to Lee. Still whispering, I mutter, "Same here, I'm afraid."

Suddenly, Porter taps Lee on the shoulder. After getting our attention he points up toward a corner of the ceiling. Though it's painted the same bland white color, he's spotted a tiny disk. Taking the desk chair, he moves it so that he can stand under the disk and yank it from the wall.

Hopping down, he pulls open Lee's front door and beckons two agents to come in. Pointing to the listening device, he motions for them to search for others.

Lee leads me into his bathroom. After he turns the sink taps on full volume, he mutters, "First he sends some kid in to seduce me, and now he's listening in on our conversations and blocking any incoming frequencies! Since when is blackmail normal behavior for our publicly elected officials?"

"I got the same treatment from my concierge, Ken. I was much less kind. My way of saying 'thanks but no thanks' left him in tears."

"Wait...*Lassiter is trying to entrap you too?*" Lee rolls his eyes.

I nod. "The fact that he's trying to blackmail us goes a long way to proving he's a Russian asset or...well..."

"Or what?" Lee asks.

"Nothing." Telling Lee about Broken Wing breaks ghost protocol.

I shrug. "We've got twenty-four hours to placate our very sick but very cunning host. I'll put on my hunting togs. I suggest you do the same. Knock on my door and we'll walk down together."

Lee nods, but his mind is elsewhere.

I get it. This place is steeped in bad mojo.

I don't need to worry him that whatever Wilbur has in mind for him isn't half as bad as what it is for me, especially now that I've rejected his first sacrificial lamb.

I pray that Wilbur takes the hint and ends whatever other nonsense he has in mind.

WILBUR'S SHOOTING range is made up of haystacks in a field placed at varying distances from the shooters' line of fire. They sport different targets. Some are bullseyes. Others, graphics of men, are black cutouts on white. Some face out. Others are in a runner's stance. A few threaten the shooters with rifles of their own.

"Here's how this works, folks," Wilbur announces. "You'll notice that each stack is allotted with a specific number of points, depending on its distance and where you hit the target. The closer your shot comes to the bullseye, the better. You'll get a turn at all the targets and get to choose which of these three spots you'll stand."

"Got it," Lee says.

"Good! Pick your pee-shooter." Wilbur points to a standing rack off to one side. It's loaded with rifles. There are three of each: Sig Sauer Cross, Springfield Armory Waypoint, Savage 110 Hunter, and the Browning X-Bolt Speed.

My first choice is one of the Sig Sauers. Lee chooses a

Springfield. Wilbur grabs one of the Brownings, then turns to me. "Ladies first, of course. Pick your spot, then take a shot. We'll rotate from there."

I choose the middle space. My first shot is at the farthest target. It's a bullseye to the heart. When the bullet hits the haystack, it shakes slightly.

Impressed, Wilbur whistles. "Well, what do you know! We have a ringer!"

Lee goes next. Like me, he also shoots from the middle and aims at the same target. The shot hits the target between the eyes: a lower score, but it ain't shabby.

Wilbur follows our lead: same stack, same spot, but his bullet hits the target's groin. He hoots, "Bullseye!"

Lee looks askance. "Seriously, Wilbur? That's where you were aiming?"

"Why not?" Our host counters. "It's the most vulnerable part of a man. And you can't feel the pain if you're dead anyway."

Based on Lee's dismay, Wilbur's made his point.

And so, it goes. My next target is on the left side of the field. This time I take a Browning. Again, a bullseye to the heart. Lee follows. He too aims for the heart, but it's off-center by a couple of inches.

Wilbur's still goes for the dangly bits, but I notice that my steadfast aim has lessened his joy of the game.

By our fifth shots, the senator is deadly serious. Proof: he too aims for the heart—and he hits it.

During my eighth shot, the stack not only shudders but a yelp is heard.

I ask, "What was that?"

"Raccoons like to nest in the stacks," Wilbur explains. "You scared one off. Good riddance."

"I wonder if we'll find both bullets, or did they go right through the stacks and into the field," I muse aloud.

"The stacks surround bales," Wilbur explains. "But don't you worry your pretty little head about the bullets. The staff will collect them when they put up the new targets. By then, we'll have tallied our scores."

Neither man wants to give up until the last stack is hit.

Afterward, Wilbur asks, "What say we go another round?"

"Sure, why not?" Lee declares.

I don't know if they're being competitive or if, like me, Lee would rather stay out in the open and with a gun in his hand. At least out here, if our host pulls anymore stunts, we can retaliate—

And no one can say it wasn't an accident.

Lee and I have each other's backs. Even Wilbur can see that.

It's now five o'clock. As we enter the foyer, Wilbur informs us that cocktails will take place at seven-thirty, before dinner, This gives us time to shower.

Lee and his Secret Service detail head to his room. Before I can follow, Wilbur takes my arm. *Yuck.*

"I hear you're an art lover," he declares. "And that you collect the works of John Singer Sargent."

"Yes. You're right on both accounts." I've got a 50-50

chance that he may have read that about Ruby, so I play along.

"Then you'll love the one I own. It's there, in my study." He points down a different hall.

The study is a beautiful room. Walls not lined with books to its tall ceilings are knotty pine like its floor. Between two facing settees is a beautiful oriental carpet. Its coffee table's centerpiece is a Remington cowboy on a bucking bronco.

Wilbur points to a small oil painting behind his desk. Its subjects are two birds. I walk over to it for a closer look. It truly is mesmerizing despite the fact that one of the birds is dead on the floor.

It also has a broken wing.

I hadn't realized that Wilbur has sidled so close that he can whisper, "It says it all, doesn't it? About our mission, I mean."

I now have proof:

Wilbur is a Broken Wing member.

He exclaims, "Aiden's generosity knows no bounds!" I mean, let's face it—whoring out his wife for our cause is truly the ultimate sacrifice. He shows true genius for realizing that whether POTUS wins or not, her Veep will be in our pocket and do our bidding." His eyes roam over me. "Not to worry. When you seduce him, the cameras will be rolling to catch each little thrust, every damp lick, all the howls and grunts..."

Just thinking about it makes him double over with a groan. "*Damn—now* look what you've gone and done! Why, you've wet my whistle, and you didn't even have to blow on it!"

I slap him so hard that he reels backward.

Angrily, arms raised, he turns toward me—

But he stops himself. Heaving, he mutters, "Save that passion for Chiffray." The thought sends him into a fit of giggles.

I run back to my bedroom.

When I calm myself, I go out into the hall. Smiling at the three Secret Service agents who guard Lee's door, I give it a knock.

Porter opens it. After exchanging pleasantries, he lets me enter.

I can't even imagine how Lee will react to my proposition.

Chapter 9

Disinformation

Disinformation is defined as "the deliberate creation and spreading of false and/or manipulated information that is intended to deceive and mislead people, either for the purposes of causing harm, or for political, personal, or financial gain."

Sadly, advances in the field of Artificial Intelligence have lowered the barrier to produce disinformation. Its forms include misinformation and deepfakes, once and for all making the premise that "If it looks like a duck, swims like a duck, and quacks like a duck, it probably is a duck" a misnomer.

A more apt animal analogy is "wolf in sheep's clothing."

"You're teasing...right?" I can't blame Lee for not believing his ears.

"I wish I were." I stop my pacing to face him.

"I get it…" Now Lee is pacing too. "But..When Jack finds out what we did…"

Lee doesn't have to finish that sentence, since we both know what he means: Jack will hate Lee even more.

He'll hate me too.

And he'll leave me, once and for all.

"So, fake it," Porter suggests.

Lee's head swivels to him just as quickly as mine, not to mention is jaw has also hit the floor.

Porter adds, "If bad porn actors can do it, how hard can it be?"

I glance at Lee to find him staring back at me.

"I guess…we can," I concede.

Lee sighs. "Okay then… But… the moment it's over, *we are out of here.*"

Porter nods. "Mrs. Spencer, since Wilbur has the cameras in your room, I suggest you return there now. Lee will follow shortly, from the hallway. So that Lassiter believes you've followed through, Mr. Chiffray's security detail will move to guard your door as well."

"Got it." I take off.

I go to my suite's bathroom. After taking off all my clothes, I put on a bathrobe.

In one of it's pockets, I slip a liquid soap dispenser.

Five minutes later, Lee knocks on my door.

FOR ANY EYES WATCHING, Lee's security follows its usual protocol: Porter walks through my suite to make sure Lee and I will be alone. He and two other agents will guard my door.

The moment it is shut, I pull Lee into an embrace.

Then we kiss:

Not bad...

But not Jack.

Despite this, to make this work, I'll have to pretend he is.

That does the trick. In no time, the heat of the moment takes over. Still kissing, we move to the bed, all the while stripping down;

All the while, faking what we feel.

At least, I'm faking it. When we're naked, it's obvious that Lee isn't.

Maybe it's for the best because *it's show time.*

I groan: not because of what I feel for Lee, but at the thought of Jack. Will he forgive Lee?

More to the point: will Jack forgive me?

I HAVE a new respect for cinematic sex scenes.

To do them right, the actors must forget that they are being filmed. Even more disconcerting, they must ignore the fact that they are being watched by relative strangers who pass judgement on their sexual prowess:

Where they put their hands or their mouths, and even what sort of dirty talk they prefer.

Who's on top, what gyrations they do to keep their partner at peak performance, and the intensity of their moans.

And then there's the timing of their orgasms. Is it loud enough to rock the rafters, or so soft that it sounds like a raincheck on some future fun and games? If it is a whimper, does it signify disappointment, or perhaps self-loathing?

How often do partners share satisfied sighs? I suppose it depends on the partners and their prowess.

Specifically, when not under duress—

Like we are now.

Our moves hit all the erogenous zones: the back of the head, the nipple, the curve of the ass. All the while, Lee struggles to keep from giving in to the ultimate move: penetration.

He knows he won't be able to control its ultimate response:

Orgasm.

But then the inevitable happens: as dick rubs against cunt, the latter aches and shivers in anticipation of receiving the former, which has now grown to its longest and hardest state.

As he looms over me, Lee's eyes are closed. Is he trying to forget whom he hovers over? If so, from what I can feel, it doesn't soften him.

At the same time, his thrusts are nowhere near me.

When he whispers, "countdown from eight," I now know the stage direction for our playacting:

Eight...

Seven...

Six...

Five...

Four...

Three...

Two...

One...

In unison, we groan. We shudder. We collapse in each other's arms.

When Lee rolls off, he's damp all over.

He slips the liquid soap dispenser into my robe pocket. I take it he didn't need it.

For him, it was the worst wet dream ever.

Turns out that faking it is just as exhausting as the real thing. Worst yet, I must be hallucinating because it seems Wilbur is also in the room.

What nerve! He's come in through a secret door.

Lee frowns, "*What the... hell, Lassiter!*"

"I'll let Mrs. Spencer do the honor of telling you about our secret club—of which you are now its newest member."

Lee turns to me. "Do you care to explain, Ruby?"

I shrug. "Lee, darling, you're now a member of Broken Wing, an organization that Aiden and I founded. Its members have one goal: to unite our country—and others around the world—into an autocracy that works for all."

Lee's face loses all its color. "Why would you sabotage Libby this way?"

"Isn't it obvious?" Wilbur sighs at his stupidity. "She's incorruptible—unlike you, thanks to Mrs. Spencer's comely wiles." He pinches my cheek—much too hard. "Why, anyone can see by the way you pant after Ruby that she's all you want."

Lee turns away.

"One last thing." Wilbur goes to a closet. Inside is an

oven. He opens it and pulls out a poker. Its flat end is in the shape of the Broken Wing insignia. From its glow, it is already hot.

"Ruby, being that you're now the most intimate of all of Lee's friends, what say you do the honors?"

I shrink against the headboard.

"Never mind. I'll do it myself."

Before Wilbur can pick it up, a gun goes off:

Porter's. The bullet hits the wall just a few inches above Wilbur's head.

"What the hell?" Wilbur's scream is pitched so high that I'm awed we can't hear dogs barking.

"I thought I heard an unauthorized voice." Porter glares at Wilbur. "Senator, accidents have a way of happening to those who overplay their hand. If I were you, I'd get the hell out. Whatever you have in mind, Mrs. Spencer can take care of it."

Wilbur sees the look in Porter's eyes. He's out the door in a nanosecond, slamming it behind him.

Porter reaches into his pocket. With sleight-of-hand, he slips me a slim see-through disk. It's the Broken Wing tattoo.

Lee gets to fake it too? Grrrr...

"Sir, the bathroom is cleared for this, um, initiation." That's Porter's way of telling us that there are no cameras in there.

Wrapping my robe around me, I pick up the poker and join Lee in the bathroom.

After Porter secures the tattoo, Lee lets out a bone-chilling groan.

In the meantime, Porter has scooped up Lee's clothes.

He hands them to his boss. "Let's give it twenty minutes, then head for the convoy." Turning to me, he adds, "Ma'am, feel free to freshen up before joining us."

I nod and hurry back through the door to my suite.

―――――

"Perfect timing, Aiden! You're back just in time to hitch a ride with Ruby and Lee—who, I'm happy to report, is now just as true blue to you as your beautiful wife." Wilbur puts his arm around his waist and gives me a squeeze.

Lee winces at the jibe. As for me, it's all I can do to hold back my bile.

Jack shrugs. "I'll be the judge of that." His tone sets Wilbur straight: *Don't assume anything.* "Ruby will fill me in on how well you assisted. Not to worry. She grades on a curve."

Wilbur bites his tongue. Forcing a smile, he says, "Next time, I hope you'll join us. I promised I'd take her hunting. She'll love that even more."

To my ears, Wilbur's murmur is a death sentence.

"Sounds like fun!" Jack is too enthusiastic. I stifle the urge to pinch him as a warning to take it down a notch.

"Any husband of Ruby's is a friend of mine." Wilbur taps my nose. "Now, lean in for a kiss, darlin'."

Aggghhh!

And yet, I play along—

Only to get Wilbur's deep-tongue dive.

I bite down hard enough that he gets the message: BACK OFF.

If there is a next time, I'll be aiming at one "critter" only: Wilbur.

"WHAT HAPPENED BACK THERE between the two of you?" Jack has waited until we're a few miles down the road before questioning Lee and my mutual silence.

Nothing!" We say in unison. Lee stares at me before quickly looking away. He's just as mortified as me.

"Come out with it," Jack declares. "I can cut the tension with a knife."

Silence.

Jack prods, "So, Ryan will be read in, but I won't?"

"I don't expect Ryan will be half as angry as you at what went down," I mutter.

Lee guffaws. "Knowing Ryan, he'll be pleased as punch."

"Damn it! Just tell me what happened," Jack insists.

"You of all people don't want to know," Lee warns.

"Unbelievable!" Jack exclaims. "So, I have to wait until we get back to the Watergate?"

At that point, the privacy panel between us and the driver opens. Porter, who's sitting shotgun, says, "Only if you behave yourself, Craig. Because after what we've been through, I'm in the mood to shoot someone. If it's you, so be it."

Jack throws up his hands. "Okay, now I have to know!"

Porter thinks for a moment. "Sure." He pulls out a set of restraints. "As soon as I put these on you."

Jack frowns. "Why?"

"Because I say so. Otherwise, let it go." Porter stares at Jack.

My husband blinks first. Then he holds out his wrists.

I wait until he's cuffed and then I take a deep breath. "I guess you'd call it cosplay."

Lee shakes his head. "More like puppeteering."

"Only we were the puppets," I add. "Wilbur's."

"And he was one sick fuck," Lee interjects.

"One sick, manipulative, lying dirty old man fuckwit," I proclaim.

Jack's eyes shift from me to Lee. "Enough with the polemics. Where are you going with this?"

"As I was saying, it was cosplay—"

"Yeah, yeah, I got that part." Jack looks heavenward. "Puppets, sick fuck, dirty old man—"

"Because Wilbur knew Libby can't be corrupted, should she be re-elected, this group you now head up—Broken Wing—is to blackmail me into being its puppet instead," Lee explains.

"What form did his blackmail take?" Jack asks.

Lee hesitates. Then: "'Ruby' and I pretended we were making love. That way, if Libby is re-elected, Broken Wing can blackmail me to undermine her platforms from within."

Jack's silence scares me. Finally, he says, "I've got to admit it's a brilliant way to kill two birds with one stone." He leans back. "So, how realistic was your so-called cosplay?"

"Well..." I shrug. "I'm no Scarlett Johanssen."

"And I'm certainly no Chris Hemsworth," Lee adds.

"You can say that again," Jack mutters.

Angrily, Lee moves toward Jack.

"Sir," Porter growls, "*SIT BACK.*"

Lee glowers but does as he's told. "However, we were... um, realistic enough to fool Wilbur."

"Is that so?" Jack's stare makes me blush. His gaze shifts to Lee. "So, Chiffray, you mean to say you kept your powder dry?"

"I..." Lee's face heats up.

The last thing Jack needs to know is that Lee couldn't hold back.

"To fake out Wilbur, I brought liquid soap into the bed with us," I explain. "Not to worry, Jack. Nothing happened between Lee and me. I assume you can say the same about you and Gabriella?"

Jack starts to say something, but then shuts his mouth, shrugging instead. "At least I know she's not in Broken Wing."

"Oh!..." Yes, I'm disappointed. At the very least, that would make Jack's time worth the effort. "Perhaps she's FSB?"

"Not from the devices I scanned. But hey, Don, you earn a Brownie points for that sly attempt to cast shade." He smirks. "Now, Lee, a word of caution. Despite your failure to launch, one of these days that smut tape will surface. Whether it's because the other side's poll numbers prove that Libby is wiping the floor with Broderick—who we already know is a Broken Wing member—eventually the video will be released publicly, and—"

He's interrupted when Porter opens the privacy panel. "There was an explosion at Libby's D.C. Campaign head-quarters!"

"Was she there?" Lee asks.

"Yes! We're hearing there were multiple injuries—and some deaths."

"How is Libby?"

"It's too early to tell. We're making a detour to Walter Reed."

The words are barely out of Porter's mouth before the limo makes a U-turn.

I'm tossed against Jack, and then against Lee.

Story of my life.

Chapter 10

Débâcle

A sudden event of destruction and great loss is known as a débâcle.

Take note! This word encompasses not just one, but two (count them: TWO) umlauts, so it must be important. Remember this for the next time you need guidance for putting your life in perspective.

THE OPERATING SUITE at Walter Reed Army Medical Center in which Libby fights for her life also has several lounges. One is specifically assigned to Executive Branch personnel and their security staffs.

It houses several SKIFs. Lee, Jack, and I are in the largest one as we talk to Ryan, Marcus, and the rest of our mission team, who are still at the Watergate.

"The doctor has read me in on Libby's condition," Marcus explains. "Seven campaign staffers were killed, and another twenty-two injured. Because POTUS was on a call in the upstairs conference room SKIF, she survived, but her injuries are categorized as critical. Libby is still unconscious, but she's expected to live."

"In what condition?" I ask.

"It's hard to say," Marcus admits. "We'll know more when she comes out of her coma. It's a given that physical therapy will be needed."

"Will she suspend her campaign?" Jack asks.

"Considering the election timeline and the uncertainty of Libby's condition, Gabriella is advocating that the party invoke the 25th Amendment as soon as possible. She's also rallying votes from Congress to have Lee endorsed immediately as Libby's logical successor."

Lucky Lee.

From the look on his face, my sarcasm aptly expresses his misgivings for having accepted Libby's offer to be her running mate.

"I...I don't know what to say," Lee says. "I accepted because I support POTUS's policies. But that's just it: she wants, and deserves, to be in the White House—not me. Gabriella tells me I'm being too modest, and that having accepted the Veep position, I knew it was possible that something like this could happen. Still, the odds of a President vacating their term while still in office is very rare."

"As things stand now, no matter how long Libby is out, it's now your turn up to bat, guy," Jack declares.

"At least we now know why Broken Wing was working so hard to blackmail you, Lee," Ryan points out. "If Libby dies, they control the new POTUS—*you.*"

Lee sighs. "So...now that I've inherited Libby's saboteurs,

what must we do next to take them down—hopefully before they kill me?"

"They won't," I reply. "Because of your supposed relationship with Ruby—and with Aiden as the leader of Broken Wing—you are now its puppet."

Lee's eyes drop to the floor.

"With the Spencers' D.C. central computer farm now disabled, we can move on to its Palm Beach doppelgänger," Ryan adds. "We assume it too holds a Doomsday server farm. If so, Abu is up to the task of disarming it."

Abu nods confidently.

"The estate there should be just as sumptuous, and the perfect place to wine and dine the candidates who are compromised—including Lee, when his time comes to call on 'Aiden' hat in hand."

Jack puts his hand on Lee's shoulder. If it's a sympathetic gesture, Lee's wince proves he ain't buying it.

I'll let Jessica know that we're to be wheels up in two hours." Ryan glances over at Dominic. "By the way, Jody will be hitching a ride with us so that the red carpet is properly rolled out."

"Too bad Carol won't be there too," I tease.

Ryan blushes. "She mentioned she was due some vacation days. I suggested that she wait until this mission is over."

Smothering a grin, Abu declares, "Then the sooner the better, right boss?"

For his sake, I'm glad Ryan didn't rise to the bait. With this mission being far from over, our boss is ornery enough as it is.

ACME'S PLANE is an hour outside of North Palm Beach County General Aviation Airport when Emma calls.

"I'm putting you on speaker," Ryan informs her.

"The first bit of news," Emma begins, "is that Acme's forensics team was able to lift a second print from the business card in Chuck Randall's jacket pocket. It belongs to Gabriella Calloway. Analyses of local security cameras show her arriving and leaving through an alley behind the coffee shop."

"In other words, she didn't want to be seen with him," Jack points out.

"For good reason, I suppose. Having stepped down as Veep, his clout was nil," I reply.

"We've already determined that Randall was a Russian asset. This is yet more proof that Gabriella may be too," Ryan insists. "Still, we'll need concrete evidence. It's time to turn the screws. 'Aiden' can do it."

I snort. "He *has* been screwing her."

"Ryan meant it as a metaphor," Jack retorts.

"And yet, you've risen admirably to the occasion," I huff. "Between Kellie and Gabriella, I'm surprised your balls aren't black and blue."

"Enough with the carping, folks!" Ryan stalks the plane. "Speaking of Kellie, she's in route to Palm Beach as well."

I turn to Jack. "Did 'Aiden' mention he'd be meeting with Broderick?"

"No, because 'Aiden' is doing no such thing," he retorts. "If she heard it from anyone, it must have been wishful thinking on Broderick's part."

"I guess that means Kellie also wants more face time with 'Aiden,'" I reply.

"Or she wants to make sure Broderick gets more bedtime with Ruby," Jack retorts.

"To do that, she'd have to make sure she keeps you busy too." I clap my hands slowly. "Lucky Aiden!'"

"Enough with the taunting, Mr. and Mrs. Craig!" Ryan snaps. "Though, in hindsight, it does allow Acme to turn up the screws on Kellie too. Jack, you'll refuse to see her."

Jack perks up. "Gladly. But why?"

"It'll make her think she's losing you to the competition—"

"She is," Jack retorts. "To *my wife*."

Yep, that earns him a few brownie points.

"—and then she'll pull out all stops," Ryan continues.

"Oh...yeah." Jack rolls his eyes. "Great." He glances at me.

"Hey," I tell him. "It's better than being branded."

"True," he concedes.

"I have even more intel about Two Buck," Emma reminds us. "There was close to thirty million dollars in Randall's Dubai bank account. After chasing the source around the world, we tracked it to a Russian oligarch's shell company."

"That certainly verifies his treason," Ryan responds. "Great work, Emma. Pass that along to Acme's ComInt and FinTech teams. Now, let's take down the terrorists once and for all."

Jack takes my hand. Like me, he's hoping this mission ends sooner than later.

THE SPENCERS' oceanfront estate is a mini-Versailles.

"The view is fabulous, but this south Florida humidity is wreaking havoc with my hair," I exclaim.

"Indubitably! I've used twice the amount of gel I normally need to keep my cowlick in place," Dominic grumbles. "It's a bit of a ding dong—"

"You have a cowlick? I've never noticed." Jack walks over to investigate. "Ah! Yes, I see it now—as well as your bald spot."

Dominic leaps up, "I say, if memory serves, one of the bathrooms has a hand mirror with a magnifying glass!"

"Ruby's," I confirm. "Since I have no such paranoia, feel free to take it with you."

"Ah! So that's why you've yet to address those tiny... or more honestly, *not so tiny* crow's feet. Should the time come when you're ready to face the obvious, I can recommend a top rate plastic surgeon."

Drat! By the time I toss my sandal, his noggin is already out of range.

THE MANSION HAS SO many rooms that, two hours later, we still haven't found Aiden's server farm.

After joining Abu in a floor-by-floor search, we then split up, retracing our steps, all the while tapping on each room's walls, bookcases, closets, and cubbies.

Finally, Abu shouts for us to join him. We find him standing in a bathroom's walk-in closet. A stairwell is tucked behind shelves holding stacks of towels.

We follow where it leads: deep underground. The

tunnel's angle is understandable, considering that Florida's heat and humidity would destroy the servers.

Finally, the stairwell ends at a large double door. It opens to a room that is as large as the mansion's footprint.

Abu's whistle is low and long. "Taking this down is a full-week's job!"

"We'll save you a few plates of canapés and a good bottle of wine from the party," I promise.

As he strips off his shirt, Abu retorts, "Better yet, why not let me play host while you swelter down here?"

"By the way, one guest who RSVPed immediately was Broderick Page," Jack warns me.

"Ooooh, lucky me!" I stick my finger down my throat. "I'll be surprised if he has the nerve to show up here after he burned me."

"I'll bet it was the biggest turn-on he's had all month," Jack teases. "Maybe you should ask him for some quid pro quo. You know, get him to agree to being hogtied, and then you can chop off some ounce of flesh."

"Great idea—like, say, his meat and two veg. Talk about doing all of womankind a big favor!"

Jack laughs. "Jenny would probably appreciate it too." He takes my hand. "We only have an hour more before Jody will want to dress us up like her own personal Barbie dolls. What say we take a nap...or something?"

"I do like the 'or something' suggestion," I admit. "There's a cabana by the pool. Care to join me?"

"I thought you'd never ask," Jack takes my hand and pulls me that way.

As TEMPTING AS SLEEP IS, we use our time to rediscover who we are together.

Knowing that soon enough we must give of ourselves to those we despise, we now focus on the tried-and-true ways that block out this despicable task.

Our lips roam freely, offering up gentle kisses. Our tongues follow up: probing erogenous zones and lapping up the dampness that seems to appear magically in these tender places.

Our hands tap, tug, and pat: delicately at first, but then we discover our fingers have minds of their own. When a thumb finds the opening it seeks, we groan with pleasure. At their best, our fingers are as agile as a concert pianist's on a keyboard.

Instead of hearing rapid trills, our hearts beat even more quickly from their erotic thrills. Legs tangle. Bits and breasts dangle. Each thrust is sheer lust.

Have I left you no doubt that love is poetry in motion?

On the other hand, hate is inevitably expressed through prose: always with ugly words describing abuse, or pain, or derision. The worst words terrorize our minds.

As Jack and I rise from our lust nest, our sighs don't reflect these few fragile moments of pleasure but the darkness we soon must face.

More so, the mission we must complete.

The sooner, the better.

THE PALM BEACH neighbors eager to meet the Spencers are mostly fawners, gawkers, and insular gossips. 'Aiden' and I aren't giving them much fodder to dissect. Instead, we rotate around the room, quizzing them on their favorite subjects.

Not surprisingly, it turns out to be themselves. Forget paddleball. Their favorite sport is one-upmanship: why their you-name-it status symbol is newer, bigger, and better than the guy's down the block.

While the catering staff plies them with food and drink, they try to endear themselves to us with the latest gossip about each other, whom they know intimately—or think they do.

Our one-word responses are the telltale sign that we aren't impressed—or even worse, bored with them.

To save face before others, they wave to someone across the room. It's an exit strategy we welcome.

And yet, they'll never let on to their frenemies that they failed to befriend us.

The Pages arrive late so that the senator can make an entrance. He sports a golf tan. Like his stubble, his full head of run-your-fingers-through-it hair is blond and naturally sun-kissed.

They've come with Kellie and another male guest. Acme's facial recognition software has him placed in no time. "He's a Russian operative," Emma divulges. "His cover is that he's a mink wholesaler."

"By the way, yet again, Kellie didn't have any mobile devices on her," Abu adds.

"That's strange," Ryan replies. "And it certainly doubles her chances of being in Russia's pocket. Even more reason for Jack to say yes to a private meeting. Jack, if she doesn't offer, you will."

"Yeah, okay." The weariness in my husband's voice is all

too obvious. Still, he forces a grin onto his lips as he waves over these late arrivals.

At least Jack covers his disdain better than Jenny. She glowers at the sight of me. It doesn't help that Broderick practically runs to my side, leaving his Russian buddy to paw her all over.

"Why would anyone wear a mink in Palm Beach?" Emma wonders. "It breaks forty degrees like, what, two days out of the year?"

"You don't need to wear it just because you own it," I reply. "It's the thought—your neighbors', not yours—that counts."

She snorts. "Ah! got it."

In no time, the Pages are front and center. After giving "Aiden" a hale and hearty handshake, Broderick leans over to me and whispers, "May we talk in private?"

"Another time. I must play hostess." My clipped tone has him wincing, but he won't be deterred. While 'Aiden' converses with Jenny and their Slavic sidekick, he pulls me into the hallway.

"Ruby, level with me. Is Aiden freezing me out?"

"What gives you that idea?"

"He never returns my calls, for one thing."

I find this odd, too, though I'd never let Broderick know that. If anything, Jack would meet with him, if only to record further evidence of his treason. Once exposed as a member of Broken Wing, his party could replace him.

"And although you claim he didn't mind that I branded you, I can't help but feel that he may be somewhat upset about it," Broderick opines.

Dude: *DUH! Ya think?*

"I let Aiden know it was a bit disconcerting to have such an intimate act administered by...well, a lackey like yourself," I admit. "Frankly, it was beneath me to allow it."

His eyes grow wide with fear. "Dammit, I thought so! Level with me, Ruby: are the Spencers going to back Lee's candidacy instead of mine?"

Because I'm having too much fun watching him grovel, I ask, "What would you do if I said yes?"

"I... I'd do anything! Anything you ask!"

"Anything at all?"

"Yes... YES! I know I've played the gentleman up to now, but I meant what I said about my...*my prowess.*"

"We all know your reputation precedes you." *As a philandering, whoring pig.*

"Perhaps we should have another rendezvous." His suggestion reeks of desperation. If I'm lucky, it'll soften any attempts to get it up.

And yes, I'd laugh long and hard. He deserves to be taken down a peg or eight.

I retort, "Alright... as long as I'm the one holding the branding iron. You know, quid pro quo and all. Ooooh! I know! I'll brand you as all mine with a private love tattoo."

Broderick flinches. "If... that's what it takes, so be it."

"Shall we, then?"

"Here...and *NOW*?" The blood drains from his face.

"It's the only way to prove your sincerity. We both know it."

"Then... Yes, okay."

I stroke his cheek. "Follow me."

He looks back at Jenny. Instinctively, I do too. Her face

moves through a kaleidoscope of dark emotions: jealousy, shame, desolation.

He ignores it, opting instead to take my hand and pull me into the hallway.

BRODERICK OPENS every door until he finds what he's looking for: a bedroom. He carries me through the threshold as if I'm his bride and he's taking me to our nuptial bed.

"First things first," he growls. But we both know it's to be no more than a rutting of convenience followed by his branding: for him to get Aiden and my blessing, I cannot be slighted.

Needless to say, he wants the icing before the cake.

If only he knew.

More to the point, if only Jenny knew.

I'm so busy fighting off Broderick's randy antics—the way he tosses me onto the bed, then rips off the buttons on his shirt so that his washboard abs and massive chest can impress me—that at first, I don't see Jenny, standing in the doorway, backlit by the hall light. I only realize someone is there when the light gleams on the metal of her gun: a pistol small enough to fit in her clutch purse. You'd think the tears running down her face would cloud her vision, but no. She knows what she sees and where to aim:

At her cheating husband's head.

The bullet propels him forward. Blood and brains, now unleashed, fly beyond the dead weight of his body, which has landed on me.

Her scream is that of a woman who realizes she's not

only put an end to her husband's life, but to hers too. This fresh meat will have to trade in those Manolos and a closet filled with Dolce & Gabbana sheaths for jailhouse hag rags. As for her hair, no more Brazilian Court Salon touch-ups. Grown-out roots aren't a great look. Then again, who does she have to impress? Certainly not her bunky, who'll demote her from candidate's wife to cellblock bitch.

I guess all of this is going through her head, too. It's reason enough to hold the barrel of her gun under her chin and pull the trigger.

Jack gets here just in time for her encore.

Kellie, worried that her candidate hasn't been making the rounds, is with 'Aiden'. Now that she knows why, she curses up a storm. Most of what she says is unintelligible. But I do catch "I've spent too many years grooming that clown for the Big Top..." and "Damn it! Now who the hell can we get to run against Chiffray?"

By then, Jack is cradling me in his arms and Abu is shoving Kellie down the hall. At the same time, Ryan runs into the room. When he sees the carnage, he lets loose with a few choice words of his own.

At least he can't blame me for this.

Though, hell's bells, I know he'll try.

IN AN HOUR'S TIME, the mansion is emptied of the guests and Jody's staff.

Dominic offers Jody a ride back to her hotel. She's happy to take it.

We're glad too. It's been a hell of a night: perfect to spend in each other's loving arms.

They've just pulled out of the driveway when an ear-shattering alarm goes off—

Followed by an explosion somewhere deep in the bowels of the building.

As the mansion shakes, rattles and rolls, flames leap out of windows. Jack, Ryan, and I run outside. Noxious fumes gag us. The tall palms surrounding the house catch fire. As they sway, sparks are caught in the breeze.

I yelp as one lands on my arm. I'm not prepared for what happens next:

Jack shoves me into the pool.

SON OF A BITCH!

My only solace is that he jumps in after me.

When I resurface, I realize why: one of the long flowing sleeves of my gown had caught fire.

We don't see the body floating our way until we resurface:

Abu's.

I beat Jack to him, but together we lug him out, roll him onto his back, and start mouth-to-mouth. It seems like hours but it's just a few seconds until he gags: proof he's alive. Then he screams, "My hands and arms are *SCALDED!*" Holding them up, he shakes them to cool them off as he runs to the pool and jumps in again.

We stare at the mansion now engulfed in flames. Hearing the fire trucks, Ryan gets out of the pool to meet them.

"Well, one thing's for sure. The Spencers will be

renowned for throwing a party that raised the roof to Kingdom Come," Jack mutters.

True that.

Chapter 11

Nostradamus

Michel de Nostredame, the 16th Century French *physician and astrologer, is revered for his predictions about the future.*

For example, he prophesied the Great Fire of London of 1666, writing: "The blood of the just will commit a fault at London, Burnt through lightning of twenty threes the six: The ancient lady will fall from her high place. Several of the same sect will be killed."

Supposedly Nostradamus also predicted Hitler, writing: "A young child will be born of poor people..." And what does this child do? "By his tongue... seduce a great troop, and his fame will spread far beyond Europe." Yet another prediction mentions fighting 'close by the Hister'..."

And then there were Nostradamus' predictions about the bombings of Hiroshima and Nagasaki: "Within two cities, there will be scourges the like of which was never seen."

Thank goodness Nostradamus had a real job! Otherwise, he'd be just another guy standing on the corner waving a big sign and shouting about doom, gloom, and the End of Days. Proving that it's not just what you predict, but from what bully pulpit you shout it from.

JODY HAS JOINED our Acme team's flight to Silicon Valley's San Jose Airport. After Jessica announces the plane's final descent, Jody hits the phones to line up the staff she needs for tomorrow's woo-fest of tech-bro supporters to Lee's candidacy. The rest of us continue our discussion of the mission's successes and failures.

In this case, there aren't many in the first column and too many in the second.

"Like Arnie, Abu's burns are too far gone for any physical tactics that your mission may need to take down the Spencers' Doomsday device," Ryan informs us.

"I can still provide remote tech reconnaissance," Abu insists.

"Me too," Arnie adds. "Perhaps we can disable the server farm with robots."

"Wouldn't their parts malfunction in all that heat?" Jack asks.

"Oh...yeah, you're right about that," Arnie admits.

"Boss, perhaps we can contract with Mad Hacker," Emma suggests.

"Just say the word and I'll reach out to her," I say.

Mad Hacker uses her skills to assist organizations with little money but strong ideals that do right by humankind. But the bad guys want her too—including Russia—for all the money she's cost them. Or worse yet, has stolen from their oligarchs.

"No can do," Ryan barks. "And that's my final word on the issue. Now, on another note: it's time to bring home the bacon on Kellie Diller."

"With Broderick out of the picture for the opposition party, my guess is that she'll make a full-court press for Aiden's support of the candidate Libby's opposition party has chosen to replace Broderick," I reason.

"She already has." Ryan glances at Jack. "Tell her."

"Kellie is flying out here. She wants to crash tomorrow's party. Ryan suggested that I invite her to have a one-on-one meeting, but to do it at the Spencer estate instead."

Of course he did.

"She's sure to have a mobile device on her then," Ryan says.

"She hasn't thus far." I counter. "If she does have a cell on her when she meets with Jack, while he distracts her, someone needs to be there to scan and crack it. Since it can't be Arnie or Abu, I still vote for Mad Hacker."

"I second that motion," Jack adds.

"Aye, Aye," Arnie chimes in.

"I vote for that too," Abu says.

Ryan sits and stews. Finally, by minute six, he grouses, "Okay, Mrs. Craig. You have my permission to reach out to Mad Hacker. But I have one caveat: she can pass on any part of the mission she feels may put her in over her head."

Jack, Abu, and I exchange looks—

And then snicker, which soon turn into giggles, which has us laughing so hard that we must stand up.

"I don't find that funny," Ryan grumbles.

As soon as I get ahold of myself, I retort, "Yeah, well... You see, the thing about Mad Hacker is that she does everything her way. We've just got to...you know, let her do her thing."

Ryan snorts, "In other words, she's as big a pain in the ass as you."

I purr, "You have the sweetest terms of endearments." Thank goodness he's got his back to me and can't see my happy dance.

"Way to cut a rug," Ryan huffs.

Yikes! He's got eyes in the back of his head too?

No. But from where he stands, he can see me in one of the cabin's mirrors. Thank goodness! For a moment there, I thought he'd indeed made a pact with the devil.

Elated, we haven't even noticed that we're in Acme's terminal and Jessica has opened the exterior door.

"Stay safe, everyone." Ryan pats Abu's shoulders, shakes Jack's hand, gives me a kiss, then heads for the limo waiting to take him back to Acme headquarters.

All is forgiven—

Unless our op goes sideways again.

BELIEVE IT OR NOT, my way of contacting Mad Hacker is old school: the missive is to be coded, with the who, what, where, and when.

I start by creating an innocuous Reddit thread:

Looking for a lost limited-edition copy of the novel, Alice's Adventures in Wonderland by

Lewis Carroll, inscribed to Alice's mother, Edith. If you wish to sell it, I'll be at the Downtown Public Library on Saturday.

As with the novel itself, my coded requests are backward. The real Alice had a sister by that name, but their mother's name was Lorina ("who": me, because I'm a mother). The words "limited edition" provides the "what:" ("meet up"), " and "Downtown Public Library" indicates wherever she chooses. Finally, "Saturday" is code for "as soon as possible."

Within an hour, Mad Hacker's Reddit response informs me that I'm to meet her at seven tonight at Comic Con. Makes sense, since it will be crowded with so many strange creatures that, even disguised, we'll look normal.

ONCE INSIDE THE largest of the convention's sponsoring hotels, I'm one of hundreds of bun-eared, flowing-white-gown-clad Princesses Leias. I spot Mad Hacker out of the corner of my eye: though she's made up in Daenerys Targaryen garb, not much about her has changed.

It's been some time since we've last met. And despite both of us being in costume, I'd know her anywhere from the one thing near and dear to her: the hot pink-gold locket she wears. Her ardent admirers, Arnie and Emma, gave it to her when they made her their son, Nicky's godmother. It holds a photo of the little tyke.

We don't acknowledge each other. Instead, we enter an

elevator that closes before any other conventioneers can stick their light sabers between its doors and stop it.

I push the button to the floor where I've reserved a suite under an assumed name so that we can talk without being overheard.

After checking it for cameras and bugs, Mad Hacker greets me with "What's up, Buttercup?"

"Our current mission requires someone with your skillset," I explain.

"Isn't Arnie up to the task?"

"He's indisposed. While taking down an enemy state's server farm, he was severely burned."

Mad Hacker gawks. Then she tears up. "How badly is he hurt?"

"The burns are severe enough that he was in shock for three days. He's only now out of it. Abu has been pitch hitting...but"—I grimace at the thought of his plight—"he was also injured."

"I'm sorry to hear that, Donna. Server farm meltdowns are an industry hazard. I wish them both a speedy recovery." She pats my arm. "So, how may I help?"

"We've eliminated two of the farms. But one more needs to be taken down as a matter of national security. It's located in Silicon Valley. Here in Palo Alto, to be precise."

This brings a knowing smirk to Mad Hacker's lips. "Figures. Where, exactly?"

"The six-acre-square estate owned by Aiden and Ruby Spencer."

"Wow! I've always wanted to meet them." Her eyes open wide. "More to the point, I've always wanted to *hack* them."

"Now is your chance." I chuckle. "I hope you won't be

too disappointed when you find out that I'm subbing for Ruby, and Jack has the honor of pretending to be Aiden."

Mad Hacker's giggles are infectious. "Well, what do you know? Once again, I've missed them by just that much." Her right hand pinches a quarter inch of air with its thumb and index finger.

"I hate to break the news, but that will never happen. You're the first to learn that their jet crashed in the Swiss Alps. The reason is unknown, and it seems that the plane will never be found." I pause, then add, "The Spencers weren't exactly White Hat. We know for a fact that they sold to the highest bidder. In many cases, that's Russia, China, Syria, Hamas, or the Saudis. Aiden's latest offering is called the Doomsday Device."

Mad Hacker snickers. "Not very original. But at least prospective buyers get the gist of its potential." She shrugs. "Sure, count me in."

"Your usual fee?"

Mad Hacker shakes her head. "Nope. This one is on the house."

"That's very generous of you!"

"My offer comes with a caveat," she warns. "Before taking down the servers, I'd like to upload a trojan that will sweep it for any programming that may be interesting for my cause: you know, software Aiden may have created. Even programs yet to be implemented. Needless to say, I'd share any with national security implications with Acme. Does that sound good?"

"By all means." Ryan will be tickled pink.

"To protect you and the rest of Acme—as well as myself, so that my work is untraceable from Acme's many enemies—

I'll deliver the data old school: not in person, and nowhere on the property. In fact, as far away from there as possible. Any suggestions?"

I think for a moment. Then I grab a pen and paper to write down the address of Carol Wise's Watergate mailbox. "Send it here."

We shake on it.

Mad Hacker moves to the door. "After I assess what security measures have been deployed by the Spencers at their Palo Alto digs, I'll let myself in."

"When, exactly?"

"It's better that I announce myself—unseen, and to you alone—when the time is right."

"Whatever you say."

"During this operation, I'll squat somewhere in the house. You won't even know I'm there," she explains. "As a precaution against the property's built-in surveillance systems, I'll also use audio, visual, and body-heat blockers between the house and anywhere I go on the property."

"How does it work?"

"It's like Harry Potter's cloak of invisibility." Mad Hacker takes a white pager from her pocket and hands it to me. "Here's how I'll communicate with you."

"Old school, eh?"

"Yep. Unlike mobile devices, pagers work on radio frequencies. You'd have to know the one assigned to a specific pager to intercept it."

"I hate to pull you away from all these fun and games, but we'll need you as soon as possible," I explain. "There's a party at the house tonight, and"—I roll my eyes—"one of our female subjects is pushing for a meeting with 'Aiden' as soon as possible, which means she may arrive prior to the party. She's Kellie Diller, who heads up the opposition party's fundraising organization. We also know she's a member of Broken Wing. And although she's been at the Spencers' two other parties, she never brings a mobile device. Things may be different for her one-on-one meeting with Aiden—in this case, Jack."

I take it 'one-on-one' is the operative word here."

"Yep," I admit. "She'll be easy to spot because she always wears pink."

Mad Hacker snickers. "Like a Barbie doll?"

"Exactly. Ironically, she also has the same impossible measurements."

"So, she's into objectification? Wow! Talk about politics as usual. She's certainly in the right profession." Mad Hacker nods at the door. "Go on ahead. Not to worry. I'll be right behind you."

I take the hint: I'm to leave first.

Who am I to question Mad Hacker's hardline rules? Heck, they've kept her incognito from her many adversaries who practice the dark arts.

Sometimes I wish I were her.

Chapter 12

Pestilence

An infectious epidemic is also called a pestilence. A perfect example of this is the Bubonic Plague.

Shakespeare also used it to describe anger that drives one to hurting another. For example, in Othello, Iago uses it as a metaphor about manipulation when he says, "I'll pour this pestilence into his ear."

Humankind may have wiped out the Bubonic Plague, but any mean girl can tell you that undermining another's confidence with lies and innuendo is timeless verbal warfare.

"By Jove, this abode—what is it called again? ...Ah yes! 'Manu Mansion'—is bigger than Windsor Castle!" Dominic murmurs.

I'm not at all surprised that the Spencers thought to name this sumptuous estate after the Egyptian sun god's western home.

Already Jody and her party crew have made great headway creating the mansion's grounds into an outdoor adult playground. There is a Ferris wheel, a merry-go-round, bumper cars, and a house of mirrors. Booze stations are everywhere. But when Jody asks if we want courtesy psychotropics in the guests' gift bags, vehemently I exclaim, "No!"

"I didn't think so, especially if you want all the overgrown frat boys on the invitation list to take their leave while they are still able to do so under their own steam." She scribbles a note on her Jody-Do pad. "I'll make sure the invitations indicate 'BYOO.'"

What does the last O in that acronym stand for?"

Jody sighs. "'Overdose.' Not to worry, though. I'll have medics in ambulances standing by."

"Yikes! I guess money doesn't cure all ills," I declare.

"From what I've seen, it creates a whole bunch of new psychoses." Her eyes scan the grounds. "That reminds me. Just in case, I should have a few lifeguards placed poolside." She rushes off.

I head up to the main house. If Mad Hacker is already there, she'll let me know by leaving something somewhere that I'd recognize as a sign of her arrival.

Fingers crossed that the voodoo she does so well doesn't spark another inferno.

I'M WALKING toward the library. When I reach its door, I hear a woman's voice: not the one I'd hoped—Mad Hacker's —but Kellie Diller's.

Darn it! She's here—*already?*

Poor Jack.

Poor me.

If she's making her pitch to 'Aiden,' I'll have to stall the conversation to give Mad Hacker time to do her reconnaissance.

Though I try hard to raise my lips into a smile, from what I see in the closest mirror it's more of a bemused smirk.

That'll do.

I walk in to find her too close to Jack for comfort—mine and his. When I say his back is against the wall, I mean it.

As I clear my throat, she glances over.

"I hope I'm not interrupting anything." To make that sound pleasant has taken years of practice.

So did my knife-throwing skills. She may find those less pleasant; like, say, the next time we meet.

"Kellie was just..." Jack stops, as if considering the best way to spin the obvious. "She was doing her best to, um..."

"It's fairly obvious what she was doing, Aiden."

Oddly, my glare—at her—only makes her smile. "I came calling with an offer I knew Aiden would find hard to refuse."

"Do tell," I growl.

"A very large slot has opened up—"

"Poor choice of words, dearie." I shift my gaze to the hem of her too tight hot pink skirt.

Her face turns the color of a plum too many days past its prime. "What I mean to say is that the lurid circumstances of Senator Page's death have left the party with a very big hole—"

"Your, er, hole is the very last thing I wish to discuss." Since I've hit below the belt, I might as well look there too.

Kellie snarls, "Funny, I feel the same about you. And yet, my party is in this predicament because of your lascivious liaison with Senator Page, which caused his wife to take his life and hers." In three strides, Kellie is at my side. "I was able to keep your role in their deaths out of the newspapers."

"What are you seeking, Ms. Diller? A thank you? Applause? A reward?" I move so that we're nose to nose. "Thanks—I suppose." I clap slowly. "Aiden, donate to her little PAC. Then say good riddance to this rough trade once and for all."

"Ruby dearest, you have it all wrong!" Jack moves to my side. "She wants... Well, she's asking me to run against Kentfield and Chiffray."

I pause—not because of his declaration, which Acme had expected—but because I see the sign I'd hoped for:

The Mad Hacker is here after all.

The novel, *Alice's Adventures in Wonderland*, was moved from its spine-out slot. It now lays across the top of the other books on the same shelf.

THANK GOD.

If Kellie has a mobile on her, perhaps Mad Hacker has had enough time to hack it and download Kellie's messages.

I glare at Kellie. "You forget, my dear. Aiden and I founded Broken Wing for one reason: not to lower ourselves to become politicians but *to own them*. The same way *we own you*."

I ring a bell.

Jody enters the room with one of her male staff members.

"Please escort this woman out. She's not to be let back

onto the property." The tremble in my voice is real, but only because I'm excited at the thought of finally finishing this mission and going home.

The man takes hold of Kellie's arm, but she slaps it away and stalks out.

Jack groans. "That went well."

"I thought so, too."

He snorts. "I was joking. Tell you what: since you feel that way for real, I'll let you break the news to Ryan that we just blew off the perfect opportunity to get the goods on one of our prime suspects."

"We did no such thing," I counter. "Mad Hacker came through for us."

Jack looks surprised. "Are you sure?"

I point to the book that was moved. "Look at its title."

He notices the change. "Great. I love that gal."

"You'll have to stand in line behind Arnie, Emma, and me."

"I'm sure her fan club is much bigger than our Acme mission team," Jack assures me.

I walk over to the book. To my surprise, there is a bright blue pager in the slot where it was previously inserted. On the pager's screen is a message:

W:

If A announces tonight, follow through with bon voyage party.

K:

On it.

I beckon to Jack. When he reaches me, I point at it: "I'll bet you a dollar that Wilbur is 'W,' and 'K' is Kellie. They're communicating by pager, just as Mad Hacker is to communicate with us."

Jack nods. "Smart. Unlike a mobile device, a pager can't be hacked. But if you know the frequency, you can intercept its messages."

I laugh. "I guess this is Mad Hacker's way of letting us know that not only has she already figured out Kellie's modus operandi, she's found its frequency too." Something comes to mind: "Aiden must have had one as well. Possibly, Ruby too."

"Why do you say that?"

"Broderick complained to me that you'd stopped returning his messages. He was worried you were pulling your support from his presidential candidacy."

"You're right, Don!" Jack reasons. "Broderick must have communicated with Aiden via his pager, which is now part of the plane's wreckage."

I glance down at the pager's screen. "I wonder what Wilbur means about a 'bon voyage party?'"

"Perhaps he was referring to the bomb at Libby's campaign headquarters."

I shake my head. "This message was sent in the last half hour. By then, POTUS's fate was known by the world."

"There's one way to find out. Kellie asked that I announce my candidacy at the party. I told her I'll do so exactly at midnight. I'll ask her to stay afterward so that we can hammer out the press release."

"She'll agree. She loves being *hammered* by you."

"Very funny." He shakes his head. "All puns aside,

remember: we already know that Kellie is part of Broken Wing. Proving that she's also a Russian asset is our endgame. Now that Arnie can monitor Wilbur and her pagers, he'll detect their coordinates and we'll have our proof that they sent and received this message. At that point, we'll drug Kellie and take her to an Acme dark site for interrogation. When she breaks, we'll have our verification."

"Can't happen soon enough," I mutter.

Jack puts his arms around me. "I'm glad you feel that way, too. Now, please call Kellie and apologize."

"Over her dead body!"

He flinches because he knows I mean it. "Donna, like you, I want this to be over as quickly as possible."

Shite. He's right.

"Yeah, okay." I sigh. "Oh, joy. I can't wait until this evening is over."

Jack knows better than to follow me. He won't like what I have to say to her anyway, so why bother?

As I'D IMAGINED, Kellie is surprised to get my call. Then she hears my mea culpa: that I've agreed with Aiden that he should run for office on her party's ticket.

I've stunned her into silence.

In time, she mutters, "Then, of course, I'll come tonight. But fair warning: it's my job to introduce him to those who will underwrite his campaign."

"Aiden has one locked-in-stone demand: that he—and only he—makes the announcement of his candidacy, which he'll do so at the very end of the evening."

"Well…"

"No ifs, ands, or buts. If you let the cat out of the back before he hits the mic, then he'll deny it. Remember, he's doing you the favor, not the other way around."

There's a long silence. Too long.

Did I just blow the op?

"Mrs. Spencer, I'll do as he's requested. But my quid pro quo is that you keep that petulant scowl off your face the whole evening. Believe me, it will go a long way to making them pony up with donations. The more money they give, the less you and Aiden have to make up any shortfall."

"Message received," I growl.

"It will also save you from more of those little crow's feet. By the way, if you need the name of a good plastic surgeon, I can refer you to one."

The nerve of this bitch!

"I've seen his work. I'll pass."

I can't blame her for hanging up.

THE TECH BROS are loving on "Aiden" as if there is no tomorrow.

They bow and scrape and hang on his every word like schoolboys in their very own Dead Poets Society.

And Kellie is right at his side: clinging onto him, soaking it all in—and glancing down at her watch every few minutes.

Especially now that it's almost midnight.

When it's ten minutes before the clock strikes twelve, she makes her way to the nearest beverage station. She doesn't say anything to the bartender, and yet he reaches below the table and hands her two glasses of champagne.

My guess: she'll take it back to 'Aiden' so that they can raise it for a toast with the crowd after the announcement.

At that moment, the pager pings in my pocket:

I do wish I hadn't drunk quite so much…
There was a dead silence instantly, and Alice
thought to herself."

Two lines from the novel. But what the heck do they mean?

Kellie's slow saunter is not back to 'Aiden' but where I sit. "May I?" she asks.

I nod for her to join me.

She holds out one of the flutes.

Ah—

Now I get it.

"How kind," I take it. My voice is steady enough.

"Shall we toast to your new role as FLOTUS in our world order?" she says.

"Aren't you counting your chickens before they hatch?"

"*Tsk, tsk!* You'll have to melt that icy demeanor. It will be totally off-putting to voters—"

The words are just out of her mouth when the first flares fill the sky. Everyone claps and hoots. It's to be fifteen minutes of boom-boom-boom and a fireworks show that rivals any July Fourth in D.C. After all, we are in The Valley, where everything is bigger, better, and longer.

At least, that's what Valley Dwellers would like to think.

Since the commotion isn't letting up anytime soon, Kellie

raises her glass in my direction. "To the next President of the United States: Aiden Spencer," she shouts. "And to his beautiful supportive wife, Ruby."

We sip.

A half hour later, the fireworks' final sparks die out.

"Best show ever!" shouts one of 'Aiden's new sycophants.

The dude's declaration gets a hardy round of applause. But not from Kellie.

The dead can't clap.

It will be declared a heart attack. Digitalis was in the flute meant for me, which I exchanged as she nervously watched some pretty young thing with an uncanny resemblance to Daenerys Targaryen flirt with Jack.

I give Jack a thumbs-down: no need to announce his candidacy, since there isn't going to be one.

A missive comes in from the Mad Hacker. Though it too is a quote from her favorite novel, there's an obvious typo:

THE TIME HAD COME.

Past tense indeed.

Chapter 13

How to Say Goodbye to Loved Ones

When knock-knock-knockin' on Heaven's door *(metaphorically speaking), there is no easy way to say goodbye to loved ones.*

But have no doubt—YOU CAN DO IT!

Here are a few tips:

First, start off by addressing the recipients with something they know you call them frequently. (And, ideally, fondly. In other words, phrases like "You little bastards" and "You dirty son of a bitch" won't carry the day—albeit those phrases are from the heart.)

Next, sprinkle in memories you share with them. (Again, keep it light, bright, and gay. Ideally, you'll stay away from remembrances of shouting matches, divorce proceedings, or drive-by shootings.

Rule of thumb: keep in mind those very famous words from Mary Poppins, "Just a spoonful of sugar helps the medicine go down, in the most delightful way!")

And finally, face the fact that you won't have the last word...

Okay, maybe—if you're shouting loud enough that those passing by your gravesite hear you and insist that you be dug up.

Think of the look on your family's face when they hear you say, "I'm here..."

I WAKE up to find Jack already up and at 'em. He smiles down at me. "Great news! Instead of throwing Lee's donor investment party here, Jody has arranged for it to take place at one of those holography funhouses."

"Sounds like it'll be a shit show," I reply.

"My sentiments exactly," Jack declares. "But by holding it off the premises, Ryan and Dominic can still scan the devices of our party's attendees and relay the data to Acme ComInt. In the meantime, Mad Hacker can stay here and continue searching for the server farm undisturbed."

I nod. "Great points, both."

Jack shrugs. "Hopefully, she won't set off something that takes this place down too, and her with it."

I wince. "If anything happened to her, I'd feel awful."

"You and me both. Thankfully, thus far she's proven to be savvier than Acme's operatives in eluding Aiden's numerous electronic trip wires. At least she won't have to worry about others getting in the way of whatever it is she has to do." He takes off toward the bathroom.

"Speaking of Mad Hacker," I call out. "there's something that—"

The pager vibrates in my robe pocket. I pull it out:

...*all I know is, something comes at me like a Jack-in-the-box, and up I go like a skyrocket!*

Mad Hacker is warning me about something...
And it's something she doesn't want me to tell Jack.
About the Doomsday device.
Time to change the subject. "I guess you're right. So, what time do we have to be at the funhouse?"

"Eight o'clock," Jack replies. "Jody's crew will be there several hours prior. She's left our costumes hanging front and center in our closets."

I tweak his nose. "They aren't costumes, silly boy! They're expensive evening attire. On the other hand, everyone else will be in standard Valley wear: jeans and a tee-shirt."

"This time you're wrong," Jack replies. "Because it's holograms, cosplay is the order of the day."

"What a shame! The way that Aiden Spencer's minions worship him, he's becoming the tech bro fashion trendsetter."

Jack looks heavenward. "Better 'Aiden' than me."

"By the way, Emma confirmed that the coroner declared Kellie Diller's cause-of-death a heart attack," I divulge. "If we're lucky, we'll get a few days' break before Gabriella comes wooing—which should also mean she'll ask if Kellie got around to asking you to run as their candidate for POTUS."

"Per Ryan's instructions, I'm to inform her that Kellie asked and that I answered I'd consider it, God rest her soul."

"Now that truly is blasphemous!" I retort.

"Which? That she asked, or pretending that I'm tempted?"

"Neither. I was referring to her soul at rest. Ain't happening."

"A long shot, for sure," Jack concedes. "Hey, let's take a bet. What do you think Libby's party will offer to keep 'Aiden' from running as the opposition party candidate?"

"The obvious. Gabriella will play their trump card: the video they have of Lee and me." I point out. "At least he can now step down as Libby's replacement candidate—something he never wanted to be in the first place. In any event, I applaud you for not going all he-man Neanderthal on him. Seriously: the last thing Lee wants is for Eve to walk out on him."

"I wish I were as convinced about that as you seem to be."

"Of course he wants out of the spotlight!"

"At least, that's what he claims." Jack leans back. "Ah, well, it was great while it lasted."

"What exactly is great about Lee getting blackmailed?"

"I get a kick out of watching him squirm." Jack retorts. "Now that he finally got you where he wanted you—naked, in bed, and supposedly saving my life by fulfilling his dream of screwing you—he knew I'd be justified to finally take a punch at him. The fact that he couldn't rise to the occasion is hilarious! So, yeah, I can finally cut him some slack."

I can't let Jack know the truth: that the liquid soap wasn't needed as a special effect.

THE COSTUMES JODY has chosen for me range from gowns—sparkly and flowing and worn tiaras or crowns—to form-fitting bodysuits in bright colors, topped off by helmets or masks.

None are to my liking. But in the end, I choose *The Avengers'* Natasha Romanov's bodysuit. Its mask is minimal, just covering my eyes. No cape, no helmet, no glitter, and no silly accoutrements that will draw attention to me.

I'm no ScarJo, but hey, none of these dudes are Mr. America either.

And besides, I'll be there for one purpose: to see who else shows up.

Jack's eyes go wide when he sees me. "Looking great, Mrs. Craig. But your missing one thing." He points to a bin, which contains various weapons. "I suggest picking wisely. These Valley Boys are out for blood."

"Hopefully, the CGI kind as opposed to the real deal," I counter.

"To advance the process of elimination, I advise you not to conceal carry, and to keep the big bang theory in mind." To prove his point, he holds up his weapon of choice: it resembles an M134 Mini-Gun.

"Jeez, Jack! if that were the real thing—"

"Yeah, I know. I could let loose with 6000 rounds per minute." He sighs. "But since I'm expected to be the meanest, baddest, and most dangerous player in the Valley, carrying something with this baby's firepower will be expected of me." He nods toward to bin. "Go on, take your pick."

I walk over to it and scan my choices, which are many.

The replicas come in all sizes and shapes. Whereas some are iconic sci-fi fantasies (I notice a E-11 Blaster Rifle and Katniss's bow and arrow), others are historically accurate weapons of yore (a World War I Mauser Gewehr 98 hunting rifle, and a Colt M 1911).

Yet others are like Jack's: state-of-the-art and lethal.

"Are you sure these things just shoot paint?"

"Let's see." Jack points his weapon at me, pulls the trigger—

And I'm doused with water.

I sputter, "Why, you son of a bitch!"

He chuckles. "Hey, you asked for it."

I stalk out of there—

But then I return, heading straight for the bin. I'm plowing through it for just the right killing machine when one catches my eye. A tag, clipped to it, proclaims:

… it kills all the rats…

"This one." I hold it up for Jack to see.

His brow arches. "It's practically a peashooter."

"Let's find out." I aim it at him.

He ducks.

Thank goodness for that! Forget about being spritzed with a little water. From the bolt that flew out of it, he would have been stunned instead.

Having made my point, I walk out.

Jack's way of making his is to fall on the floor, laughing—

The bastard!

AS FAR AS SUSPECTS GO, the hologram funhouse is a huge success. Everyone who donated to Libby and lives within a hundred miles seems to have shown up tonight.

I look around for Jack. No surprise: he's surrounded by an adoring army of ass-kissing tech bros.

"Donna, Mad Hacker suggests you keep circulating," Emma tells me.

"Will do," I acknowledge. Like Arnie and Abu, Mad Hacker is remotely scanning and vetting attendees to see if we're being shadowed.

The words are just out of my mouth when my pager buzzes:

She's under sentence of execution.

I duck, all the while scanning those around me. When my eyes light upon Jack, I see he's aiming at me.

His shot hits its bullseye: my heart.

I'm struck with paint from his gun.

But I'm also shot from behind: voltage that stuns me.

As I fall to the ground, Jack hoots as if it's some big joke. The three guests who have been begging to be his next victim clap wildly.

'Aiden' bows, but then he aims his weapon again. "Who wants to be next?"

Doesn't he see I'm in pain?

Despite their pleas of "Me! Pick me!" he shoots at the men's feet, unaware that I'm not acting.

As they run off, he follows.

My cries, no louder than a whisper, are useless.

And yet, someone runs over. The person kneels beside me. I try to move up, to see who is holding me.

It's Darth Vader.

He lifts his mask so that I can see who's under it: Wilbur Lassiter smiles down at me. "Tag, you're it."

The second bolt brings shudders through me. Then—

Nothing.

———

"Time to wake up, my pet." I cringe at Wilbur's term of endearment.

Still, I open one eye. Thank goodness, I'm still dressed, but I'm chained to a cot in a cage. At least I'm not gagged.

"How long have I been out?" I stumble to my feet and over to the bars so that I'm face to face with Wilbur.

"Long enough for that hubby of yours to be worried." He goes nose to nose with me. "So, tell me, sweet Ruby. What should I do with you?"

He called me Ruby...

Which is good. He still doesn't know who I really am. "I assume you already have plans for me."

"You're right. I do..." He sighs heavily. "Or, I should say, I did. It included the usual fun stuff—you know, rape and torture." He rewards me with his jack-o-lantern grin. "But then I realized someone who would just love to have you for his very own."

"You mean, my husband? Not to worry. He'll readily pay your blackmail, which, I assume, will be some donation to your PAC." Congress's legal troughs can also be used for extortion. What a country.

"Nah. For what I'm thinking, why attract any scrutiny at all?"

If you mean Broken Wing, of course, Aiden and I will continue to fund it. We've discussed a bonus program—"

"Wrong again." Wilbur strokes his chin. "Unlike the Spencers, I don't need world domination to make me feel complete. I'll settle for appreciation. And trust me, because of you, I'll be greatly appreciated by Vlad."

Cold sweat rolls down my back. "Vlad whom?"

"Putin, of course. He'd be tickled pink to have something to hold over your husband—like, say, a large ransom."

Wilbur doesn't know about my history with the Russian president. I can't allow him to find out.

"Acting as Putin's lackey, eh?"

Wilbur pouts. "Not at all! I see myself as a diplomat who wishes to facilitate peace between two parties. Sometimes even more. You can't buy that kind of goodwill."

"I'm sure your cut of the deal will be large enough to buy anything your shriveled little heart desires," I retort.

He chuckles. "Sometimes as much as fifty percent! So, yes indeed."

"Why bother with Putin when you can keep all the spoils of my ransom for yourself? Trust me, your payday with Aiden will be so large that you'll no longer have to curry favor with Vlad, let alone all those petty do-nothing lobbyists."

His silence speaks volumes.

Finally, he mutters, "Let me think about it."

He walks out of the room, slamming the door behind him.

The fact he didn't touch me is a good sign: he doesn't want to damage the goods.

I WAKE from the shock of the cold water that Wilbur tosses over me.

So much for not wanting to damage the goods.

"Why—*you stupid little whore!*"

"I beg your pardon?"

"Cut the posh British accent, *Donna Craig!*"

He knows my real name. But... How?

"You've made a fool out of me, Mrs. Craig—in front of Putin!" He slaps me across the face. "You disgraced me, you... *you bitch!*"

He's close enough that I can spit blood in his face. "I'm glad someone had a giggle at your expense."

Wilbur curses as he wipes his face. When he's done, he growls, "It'll cost you a lot more than it costs me."

He turns on a monitor that faces the bed.

It shows me in bed, but not this one. There's someone on top of me. The man's face may look like Wilbur's, but the body belongs to the young dude who failed to seduce me: Ken.

And though it looks as if it's me he's raping, it's not. It's really Taffy, that young woman who put the make on Lee. I can tell by the butterfly tattoo on the back of her thigh.

"This never happened!"

"You're right. It's a deepfake. Pretty good one too, ain't it?" He crows. "I knew it would come in handy some day! Well, today is that day."

"What exactly are you going to do with it?"

"Hush, gal! Just watch it to the very end!" His eyes are riveted. It doesn't take long before he's panting. "Wait for it....*Now!*"

Fake Wilbur, washboard abs and all, rolls off his conquest. Still panting, he reaches under the bed—

And pulls out a gun. When the bullet hits her head—that is, my head—it snaps back against the headboard. The black hole made by the bullet dribbles with blood.

Real Wilbur cackles, as if it's the funniest thing he's ever seen. "Right now, the U.S. Postal Service is knocking on your husband's door with a special delivery of this Masterpiece Theater. Jack will watch it. Sure, he'll be heartbroken, but hearing how your last thoughts and prayers were for him and the kiddos will do his heart good. What he won't know is that you'll be put on a Russian submarine and on your way to one of Vlad's dachas. He can't wait to meet you in person—again. But this time, you won't be stealing anything from him. He will finally own you—his dream come true!" Wilbur crows as if he's the cock of the walk. "And it'll be my doing! Talk about a big thank you!" He leans in. "As for Jack, in time he'll forget all about you."

Wilbur is walking out when I shout, "Jack won't believe I'm dead because... Never mind."

Wilbur stops. "Because why?"

"Nothing. Forget it."

He takes the bucket and leaves the room. A moment later, he's back with it. He tosses its contents—more cold water—onto me. "Tell me, whore! Unless you want to freeze to death!"

"Okay, sure, I'll tell you." Still, I hesitate, as if my reluctance is real. "We made a pact that... that if we were ever in a terminal situation, we'd send a letter with our last thoughts. Otherwise, we'd never stop looking for the other."

Wilbur stares, chuckles, and leaves.

My sobs are silent. I close my eyes.

When I open them again, I realize Wilbur has come back. He's grinning. And he's got paper, pen, and an envelope in his hand. "Sure, okay—*write it.* Let's break Jack Craig's li'l ol' heart and make sure he's over you once and for all." He tosses the items through the bars.

As the solitary page of paper floats toward one of the puddles, I scramble for it, catching it right before it falls. I rush over to the bed with it. Leaning over the night table I write:

I'm dead, perhaps looking down on you
with all who went before us. As for
how, I
will tell you it wasn't pleasant. Should my
remains come your way,
bury me in the spot we always discussed,
As for Jeff, I know
he's taking the news pretty hard. Know that
I'll be
sending angels to watch over them all.
As for
me, tell the children they will feel me beside
them.

To Mary and Trisha, explain that in every
rush of a breeze, they'll feel my presence.
Ah, Jack, Be strong for them! You'll never
be alone.
    Have heart, my love! I'll always be at
your side until
    my memory finally fades. In the meantime,
please
    pretend I'm right there beside you. Even
at my
    funeral, you will feel is my arms wrap
around you,
    Watch for signs of me all around you. Kiss
the girls and
    him for me.

    —Your darling Donna

WHEN I'M DONE, I print on the envelope the Watergate
address and this box number:

J Craig
℅ The Watergate
Box 2722
Washington D.C. 20022

· · ·

Wɪʟʙᴜʀ ᴡʜɪsᴛʟᴇs as he strides out with it.

I lie back down on the cot but turn my head away from the camera. I'll never let Wilbur see me cry. That way, he can't record it and then replay it for his personal enjoyment.

Chapter 14

Nuclear Winter

The earth has experienced winters that were abnormally cold and dark, when smoke and dust choked the atmosphere and blocked the sun's rays.

A period such as this is known as a "nuclear winter."

Relationships have these as well. Imagine a couple out of touch with each other. Or worse, out of love.

In both cases, a nuclear winter is human made.

However, in time, the earth forgives us for our pollution misdeeds. It does this one of two ways: either we realize we're killing Mother Nature and ourselves along with it and change our dirty little habits, or our nuclear winters get the worst of us and it's "RIP, Human parasites!"

The same can be said for a spouse: they willingly work out the underlying issues so that they may forgive us.

Or they leave us.

If not, in either situation, it's the end of the world as you know it.

Solution: Let's fix this thing!

ACME CONTACT LOG TRANSCRIPTS
Date: December 14, 20XX
8:15am PT

Call Recipient: Ryan Clancy, CEO, Acme Industries
Contact: Carol Wise, Executive Director - National Counterterrorism Center

CLANCY:

It's great to hear your voice, Carol.

WISE:

Yours too, Ryan. You sent a sweet thank you note and—

CLANCY:

If I'd known you'd respond so quickly, I'd send them all the time.

WISE:

(Chuckles):

Well, then, by all means, don't hold back. I'll always look forward to hearing from you... But... Well, this call isn't just a thank you. It has to do with another missive I've received— from Donna Craig.

(SILENCE)

WISE:

Ryan? Are you still there?

CLANCY:

Yes. Just a minute, though, I want to close my office door.
(SFX: DOOR CLOSING)

CLANCY:

I'm back with you, Carol. Can you tell me who it's addressed
to?

WISE:

It's for Jack.

CLANCY:

Before you open it, can I ask that you put on surgical
gloves?

WISE:

Wait a moment while I put on a pair.
(SILENCE - 2 mins)

WISE

I've put them on and I'm opening it now. Would you care for
me to read it to you?

CLANCY:

If you don't mind, yes.

WISE:

Okay. It says... 'Dear Jack, If you're reading this...' Oh...dear!

Ryan, I think... I think I should send it to you instead, via a secure cloud.

CLANCY:
Why?

WISE:
I ... Let's just say that it is very personal and... It may be her last letter. Frankly, I feel it's for Jack's eyes only. Or at least initially.... Because... Well...

CLANCY:
Carol, what is it? What are you seeing?

WISE:
It's odd... By that, I mean, the way the lines break. As one would assume, eventually you must move to the next line. But... in this letter, the breaks seem very odd.

CLANCY:
I'll be honest with you, Carol. Donna is missing. My guess is that she was writing it under duress. I'll send an Acme courier for the original so that our organization can do its analysis. Our operative will ask for you personally. The verification phrase will be, and I quote: Docket, Apple, Sunny, Wisconsin, end quote.

WISE:
I'll release only then, promise.

CLANCY:

If I weren't so worried, I'd send you a ticket to hand
deliver it.

WISE:
Send one anyway. I'm always up for a West Coast vacation.
Especially if my host is as handsome as you.

CLANCY:
(Laughing)
Flattery will get you everything. You're on, Ms. Wise.

WISE:
Noted. (PAUSE) Ryan, do let me know how this issue turns
out... If my clearance merits it, I mean.

CLANCY:
I think you'll pass muster. My guess is Marcus would come
to the very same conclusion, considering that you may have
saved the lives of one of our ops. Much thanks again, Carol.

[END OF CALL]

ACME CONTACT LOG TRANSCRIPTS
Date: December 14, 20XX / 08:42 am
Call Recipient: Jack Craig, Senior Operative,
Acme Industries
Contact: Ryan Clancy, CEO, Acme Industries

CLANCY:

I've just received a note that was left in Carol Wise's mailbox at the Watergate. It's addressed to you, from Donna.

J. CRAIG:
Thank God!

CLANCY:

Unfortunately, Jack...It's not what you think. I'll send it by way of our secure cloud, so that you can read it for yourself. Afterward, call me back and we'll discuss our next step.

J. CRAIG
Will do.

[END OF CALL]

**ACME CONTACT LOG TRANSCRIPTS
Date: December 14, 20XX / 08:48 am
Call Recipient: Ryan Clancy, CEO, Acme
Industries
Contact: Jack Craig, Senior Operative, Acme
Industries**

J. CRAIG:

I'm on my way back to Acme to discuss this in person.

CLANCY:

Jack, if you need time...to be with the kids and tell them—

J. CRAIG:
I... I already know what to say. When I get to the office, I'll explain what I think we should do to sustain Donna's legacy.

[LINE GOES DEAD]

Chapter 15

Gaia Hypothosis

Taking its name from the ancient Greek goddess of Earth, this theory claims Earth's biological systems are synergistic, akin to the organs of a body. Supposedly, this singular entity has closely controlled feedback loops that keep the conditions on the planet within boundaries that are favorable to life.

What happens to its feedback loops when Earth gorges itself on the human equivalent of pie? (The gastronomic as opposed to the mathematic?)

Which begs the question: are humans the equivalent of a cotton candy sugar high—that is to say, all hot air and no nutritional value?

Worse yet, because of humankind, Earth is experiencing more hot air than it should.

Solution. If there was ever a time to put Earth on a diet, this is it.

A DAY LATER, Wilbur is finally back, and he's jubilant. "Your beloved got your swan song! You better believe your tall hunky hubby is devastated! Your Acme colleagues did their own memorial on the building's rooftop. Quite touching, I must say. I thought you'd like to see it. I must admit, it even had me shedding a tear or two."

The monitor flickers on. Acme's rooftop garden is in full bloom under a cloudless cerulean sky. Among the garden's kaleidoscope of colorful blooms, Acme's staff shuffle like black crows lost in a futile search for the crumbs of meaning for their colleague's senseless death at the hands of a ruthless traitor.

If only they knew.

What I see next will let me know if they do:

Jack, stoic and hollow-eyed, stands to one side. The children—Mary, Jeff, Trisha, and Evan—surround him. Tears run down their sweet faces. Emma and Arnie stand nearby. Jointly, they cuddle a silent and awed Nicky in their arms. I see Carol Wise as well, sobbing into a kerchief. Dominic is consoling Jody and MI6's Teddy Twala, whose boss, Daniela Braxdale Cuthbert, is in the pew behind them, dabbing away tears.

Ryan stands at a podium. He's reading a tribute. In the past, I've heard similar ones honoring those colleagues who have fallen in the line of duty.

And now it's my turn.

Sort of.

The sweet praises he sings about my mission successes are leavened with wry asides about my tendency to go rogue at whim, though, to Ryan's credit, he admits that, in most cases, all was well that ended well. Throughout his sermon, tears that still cling to the mourners' faces are freed to continue their slow rolls by heads shaking from bittersweet laughter.

A good time is being had by all at the expense of my life, if not my death.

At least, not yet.

I stare at Jack, willing him to give me some sign that he decoded my message and knows the truth.

But no. Instead, as Ryan's tribute ends, Jack moves to stand beside the eternal flame that signifies that I'll live on in the hearts and minds of my Acme teammates.

When he reaches it, he pulls out a letter.

Wilbur zooms in to see what it is:

My letter to Jack.

Jack puts it in the flame. For a moment it flares brightly, then dies.

Jack looks skyward—

And winks—

But just for a second.

I shift by gaze to my captor.

He didn't see Jack's reaction because he's having too much fun watching the plains of my face shift with the pain of my realization that I'm lost to those I love most.

More so, to my husband, Jack.

Wilbur walks out, cackling with glee.

ACME CONTACT LOG TRANSCRIPTS

**Date: December 14, 20XX / 08:48
Call Recipients:
Ryan Clancy, CEO, Acme Industries
Jack Craig, Senior Operative, Acme Industries
Contact: Emma Honeycutt, Acme Industries
ComInt Director**

HONEYCUTT

Boss, and Jack: I just received a missive from Mad Hacker. My guess is that it's a clue about Donna's whereabouts.

J. CRAIG

FINALLY! I've been climbing the walls, wondering when she'd reach out!

CLANCY:

What does it say, exactly?

HONEYCUTT

If we're to take it literally, it wouldn't make any sense. All her messages are puzzles, and from *Alice in Wonderland*. In that regard, she sent these direct quotes from the book in this order:

...she was up to her chin in salt water. Her first idea was that she had somehow fallen into the sea.

It's followed by:
do THAT in a hurry.

J. CRAIG:

In other words, she's being moved offshore, and time is of the essence.

CLANCY:
Despite that, we'll still need coordinates.

HONEYCUTT
She sent something else. From what I can tell, it's the link to a feed from a tracking device.

CLANCY:
Where is it headed now?

HONEYCUTT:
It's on land—in San Mateo County, here in California—but heading west, toward the Pacific shoreline.

J. CRAIG
Then it's in our current vicinity.

HONEYCUTT:
Yes, it's close to the Spencer Estate—but not for long.

J.CRAIG
I'm getting in the car now. After sending the GPS coordinates, track me via phone. I'll also wear a GPS microdot.

RYAN:
Same for Dominic and me, Emma. We'll be Jack's back-up.

HONEYCUTT:
Done. Keep an open line, gentlemen.

JACK:
Always.

[END OF CALL]

Chapter 16

Doomster

One who believes in predictions of pending doom for our planet is known as a "doomster."

Though other terms for this person include "doomstalker" and "doomsdayer," you've got to admit that "doomster" is a much hipper handle.

"How 'BOUT YOU join me for dinner, little lady?" As silent as a snake in the grass, Wilbur is again at my cage.

Sun filters through the grated window high on the wall, bathing him in light. Despite this and his angelic gesture, I have no doubt he's the devil reincarnated.

"Sure, why not?" Food is the best way to a starving person's heart.

He opens my cage with a key and then uses another to detach the chain that holds my spread bar. Despite knowing full well that its width only allows me to walk in geisha-like steps, he yanks me impatiently, then giggles when I trip and stumble to my knees.

"I'm glad one of us is having fun with this cruel little game of yours," I grouse.

Once out of the dungeon, he pulls me into a long hall. The few minions we pass scurry out of the way, their heads bowed low. Obviously, they've witnessed other unfortunates shuffling to their last meal.

One is Ken. He practically runs out of my way. He knows full well that one must see no evil, speak no evil, hear no evil, and do the evil demanded of you to avoid being a victim of the evil you've witnessed upon others.

Not to mention the pay is better than minimum wage, or so I've been told by the master of the house.

We enter Wilbur's large, elegant dining room. Its long antique table is set for two. The end seat, a throne, is where my host will regale me with his misdeeds and tall tales of derring-do-evil. My chair, to his right, allows him to yank my chain at will, and not just metaphorically.

Being my last meal, I hope it's not some diet plate of fruit and vegetables. And yes, I want dessert, and lots of it.

If I eat so much that my host becomes queasy, all the better. Should he gag on his bile, I'll provide relief: not by slapping his back but stabbing him in the heart. The ideal coordinates: to the left of the sternum, between the fourth and fifth ribs.

The thought is mouthwatering.

"You're drooling, and you've yet to eat a bite," Wilbur declares. "Here, let me cut you some of this roast." He slices away at the haunch of meat on the silver tray in front of him. "And how do you feel about liver?"

"I can take it or leave it," I admit.

"My chef is French. Trust me, the way he prepares it, you'll find it to be a delicacy like no other."

"Sure, okay, I'm game."

He giggles uncontrollably—and with his mouth open.

Well, there goes my appetite.

He takes note of my distaste, which he assumes is at the amount of food he's loaded onto my plate. And yet, he plops it down in front of me with a sigh. "What's wrong, honeybun?"

"To tell you the truth, I'm not as hungry as I thought."

"Ah, well, that's a shame." When he tosses down the carving knife and fork, they clatter when they hit the tray. You see, I've set one house rule: guests must eat everything on their plates."

"I'll do my best... But I make no promises." I lift my chained hands. "It would be easier if I didn't have to wear these charm bracelets."

"Not to worry, pet. I'll feed you myself." With the carving knife, he cuts a square of the haunch.

"Frankly, I don't like my meat so rare."

"It's rare, alright! And for good reason." He holds up the square at eye level:

It has a butterfly tattoo.

Taffy's.

I don't know what he was expecting, but for some odd reason he didn't consider his divulgence would incite his guest to projectile vomit.

His cusses come out despite all his sputtering. With his eyes closed to the horror if my bile, he can't see me wrap the lead chain around his neck. Because he can't choke and call out for help at the same time, I can goose-step him forward.

We get as far as the window before I'm pricked from behind.

I turn around.

Ken stands beside Wilbur. He holds a syringe.

My eyes flutter shut before I pass out.

I WAKE up to find myself hogtied in the back seat of a sedan.

Wilbur is driving.

I mutter, "I didn't know you were tall enough to reach a steering wheel."

"Very funny." I catch his scowl in the rearview mirror. "Everyone underestimates short men; even more so if they're older gentlemen."

"Cruelty has nothing to do with height," I counter. "It has to do with one's psychosis. And man, are you ever a psycho! Trust me on that. I've met my fair share, so I know."

"Aw, hell. I was hoping for a quiet drive," he grumbles. "But if we must engage this one last time, I'll leave you with a quote from Robert Browning: 'Measure your mind's height by the shadow it casts.'"

"Yeah, whatever." I yawn to make my point: his opinion will never matter to me.

"I hope the first thing Putin does with you is cut out your tongue," Wilbur snarls. "But I doubt it. He's a connoisseur of fellatio."

"The way you suck up, I've no doubt you've experienced it firsthand."

Wilbur is so angry that the car swerves. Because we're on an expressway, the car beside lays on its horn.

Wilbur snarls, "Dammit, bitch! I cannot wait to get rid of you—and this!" He holds up a baggie. It contains a thumb drive.

"What the hell is that?" I ask

"Did you think I'd forget your porn video with Lee Chiffray? Hardly! Vlad doesn't need a fluffer. But if there was ever something that could do the trick, it's you, doin' the nasty with a former president—who, with Russia's help, will once again be president."

"If you drive off the road now, your wish—and mine— will be granted. Or perhaps just one of ours. Fifty-fifty chance, eh? Vegas odds! What say we take them?"

"SHUT THE HELL UP!" To make his point, he swerves again. I get tossed from the back seat. This time after hitting the driver's seat from behind, I end up on the floor. No matter how hard I wriggle, I can't get back onto the back seat, let alone turn around so that I'm facing up.

Eventually, we'll get to our destination. If I'm lucky, we'll arrive before his Russian contacts. That way, it'll still be him and me.

I'm stronger, taller, and this isn't how I'm going to die.

<hr>

FINALLY, he slows down. I hear a guard's voice, waving Wilbur through some gate, but the window stays up so the man can't hear me call out.

Would he do something if he could?

As if reading my mind, Wilbur says, "Yep, he saw you.

Didn't matter. Do you know how many li'l fillies I bring through here? That dude makes more money lookin' the other way than he gets with his salary and pension combined." He chuckles. "And besides, I've always got a great stock tip for him. Quid pro quo, baby! Am I right?" He stops short. "Speaking of which: I'd be willing to forget this little rendezvous, if you were willing to, you know, bring an ol' man to tears."

"Sure, okay. Untie me and let's get at it." *As if.*

"Nah. Just wanted to see how far you'd go to stay alive."

"That's okay. I didn't mean it either. I just wanted to see how stupid you were, already knowing that you can't tell Vlad you somehow lost me on the way to meet his U-Haul truck."

"Say, what?" There's that rooster cackle again. "No, baby doll. Donna Stone Craig is going to Russia *in style*! You're arriving in a *submarine*! First class, bitch! All the way!"

"Lucky me. FYI: a first-class ticket on Qatar Air would probably get me there quicker—and less smelly. I mean, seriously: do you know how frequently—or I should say, *in*frequently—submariners bathe?"

"Lordy! I should have gagged you! You're one hell of a nag. I don't know how Jack put up with you. Past tense now, of course."

If that is meant to shut me up, he's succeeded.

Finally, we pull into a parking spot. He gets out but returns in a moment. After opening the back door, he positions something beside it. A moment later he's yanking my chain so that I fly backward. While I choke, he grabs me under my shoulders, pulls me out of my downward dog position, and rolls me into a low-sided metal dock cart.

I land with a thump, but I twist my body so that I look up. Wilbur is too busy trying to steer the cart down the dock ramp and over to his yacht to look down.

Fine with me. I'm tired of his ugly death mask of a mug.

In time Wilbur gets to his destination. The yacht is named *Monopoly Man*. How fitting. It's a fifty-nine-foot Sea Ray SLX 400.

"It's cute." I'm being cruel.

"Yep. And you should see my other boat. It's twice the size of this one."

"That's what *he* said."

"Hey, I'm serious! I keep it in D.C."

"I'll remember that when the Feds ask what else they should confiscate from you. Finders, keepers. Traitors, weepers."

Wilbur rolls his eyes. "Lady, I can't wait to toss you onto that grinder and watch it disappear into the deep."

That silences me as we glide out to sea.

About fifteen minutes from shore, he cuts the engine. As *Monopoly Man* bobs in the wake, Wilbur's VLF radio crackles from time to time, but then it goes crazy with a code. It's not Morse, but Wilbur responds to it with a message of his own.

"They're six minutes away."

Shit! If there was any time for the Cavalry to make its appearance, this is it.

But no. No sound of any engines. Just silence.

And then we see it, surfacing like a breaching whale. From its size, I gauge it to be a *srednyaya*—a medium cruiser.

It gives a coded signal. After responding, Wilbur proclaims, "Your chariot awaits, honeybuns!"

"At least undo my legs so I can walk aboard."

He thinks for a moment. Finally, he pulls a key from his pocket. As he bends down and puts it in the lock, he says, "You're right. I'd hate for one of our hosts to break his back because you're a bit more zoftig than they'd expected–"

Well now, that's cruel enough to merit my knee whacking him under his chin. Of course he spirals backwards before falling over the rail. The chains that bind us jerk me toward it too. For once, I thank my lucky stars that he trussed me up in the spread bar because it's the only thing that saves me from going overboard, too.

When I look on the deck below, I realize Wilbur isn't cussing, let alone talking, because he was strangled by the chain.

And then I hear Jack, yelling, "Donna! Donna! Where are you?"

"Over here! ... But ... *Did you come over on the Russian sub?*"

"It's U.S. Navy. I'll explain when I get there."

"You'll need wire cutters. I'm still tethered to Wilbur's corpse with a chain."

"I'm sure there's a pair onboard the sub. Be right back."

Just hearing his Zephyr moving in the wrong direction fills me with anxiety. I take deep breaths and count to sixty about fourteen times before I hear him again, but this time he's coming my way.

After heaving himself onboard, Jack uses a flashlight to signal that all is shipshape. As the submarine goes on its merry way, Jack runs to me. I try to meet him halfway, but the chain only lets me go so far. Seeing this, he picks up speed until he can take me in his arms and kisses me as if he never wants our lips to part, ever.

When inevitably, we come up for air, Jack whispers, "Never again will I let you out of my sight."

"I appreciate your sentiment, but if we're ever going to get out of here, you're going to have to cut me loose from Wilbur."

"Oops, almost forgot!" He looks over the railing. "What do you think, should we drop the corpse overboard as fish chum?"

"He had no next of kin," I reason. "And an autopsy means there will be a lot of explaining to do, especially since he's one of our illustrious elder statesmen."

Jack sighs. "Don't tell me we're sweeping his treason under the rug."

"That's Marcus's call, I guess. But you're right about the body. Since we're far enough out to sea and he's already got a chain around his neck, I vote we tie an anchor to it and cut him loose."

"I second that vote. I'll take care of it. In the meantime, as sexy as you look in that get-up, I suggest you check the cabin for something more seaworthy. And besides, no one really believes Natasha Romanov would be hitching a ride with that lascivious creep, especially when she and her main squeeze already own the Staten Island Ferry."

I salute him. "Aye, Aye, sir. And on the way back to shore, you can tell me how you happened to hitch a ride with a Navy sub."

It takes me all of ten minutes to find the perfect attire: khakis, a white button-down shirt, and a pair of sailing shoes almost my size. The pants are the right length, but Wilbur was bigger in the girth. I use a length of rope to keep them up around my waist.

I come topside with two bottled waters. Jack is about to shove Wilbur overboard. Together we do the honors, declaring, "*Mauvais voyage!*"

The anchor pulls him under in no time. From now on, he can do me no harm.

After taking a large sip, I sit back to hear all about Jack's rescue mission.

"It truly was a team effort," Jack begins. "Arnie and Abu went through all the hologram playground's security footage until they found you. It shows someone dressed like Darth Vader. He used a stun gun."

"It was Wilbur," I admit.

"Considering how short he was, I guessed as much. He had two others with him. They were dressed as Stormtroopers. They held you between them and walked you out as if you were too drunk to do so yourself. Acme then followed the car via satellite surveillance. It ended up at a large estate that's owned by a trust in the name of Wilbur's deceased mother. It's less than an hour from the harbor where Wilbur set sail to meet the submarine. Mad Hacker hacked Wilbur's security feed, his cell, and his computers. She also diverted his messages to the U.S. submarine that Ryan secured for your rescue." Jack frowns. "Unfortunately, this wasn't accomplished before Wilbur informed Vlad about kidnapping 'Ruby.'"

"I know. It was only when Wilbur sent my photo to Vlad that he was informed of my real identity," I explain. "He was told to put me on a sub that was trolling our coastline."

Jack grimaces. "I imagine Russia's supreme leader saw it

as the perfect payback for losing you when you escaped from Mason Ledbetter." The chess master, a triple agent, was the first to try to sell me to Putin.

Someday the bad guys will get the message: any attempt to separate me from my family is a losing proposition.

"I wait until after Jack steers the boat through some chop, then ask, "How did you get the sub?"

Marcus pulled in a favor," Jack replies. "It's decommissioned. The fact that Acme had the time, date, and coordinates of the Russian submarine allowed the Navy to block and capture its crew far from the rendezvous spot and send the decoy instead." He shakes his head and declares, "When Libby learns how dirty Wilbur was—not to mention the rest of Broken Wing—heads will roll."

"How is Libby doing?"

"Thankfully, she's out of her coma. As for her injuries, we'll no more in a few days," Jack admits.

I say a silent prayer for our dear friend.

The stars in the night sky look beautiful, like bright uncut diamonds scattered over an indigo velvet scarf that runs as far as the eye can see.

Jack declares, "I want this mission to be over."

"You and me both." I lean against him. "Now, straight on 'til morning, shall we?"

Chapter 17

Deep Learning

"Deep Learning" is a computer teaching method. By using artificial neural networks to recognize patterns in data, more accurate predictions will be made.

AI has also enhanced Deep Learning's possibilities. For one thing, it has improved Deep Learning's object detection and autonomous driving capabilities.

Just as importantly, AI has increased its user-friendliness with voice and image recognition.

If it sees you and the calls you by your name with a hearty "Good afternoon!" Answer back. Or, at the very least, give it a friendly wave.

Otherwise, it may spread the rumor that you're a curmudgeon.

Or worse, a bitch.

"Now that the 'Spencers' have wined and dined everyone who is a suspect and Acme is in the arduous process of analyzing all the data downloaded from their party guests for evidence of links to Russia intelligence, Emma tells me that Mad Hacker is focusing on where the Doomsday device is located." Ryan makes this announcement jointly to our Acme team and Marcus. We're on a conference call in a secure portable SKIF set up in the Clement, a local Palo Alto Hotel.

"Works for me," Dominic declares. "It may have not been noticed because I'm aces at covering for it, but truth be known, I have minimal technical acuity. If I were to be called into action as such, surely, I'd be the next to be fried like a chippie!"

Jack snorts. "Yes, we all know you're a shit tech op. Despite that, is this your way of saying you've got somewhere better to be?"

Dominic's face flares bright red. "Not at all! I'm just pointing out that my primary skillset—that of a handsome bon vivant—has been somewhat underutilized on this mission."

Jack's stare is long and hard. Finally: "Frankly, I agree. Tag, you're it to be the next honeytrap."

"Your offer couldn't be better timed, Dominic," Ryan adds. "Our final suspect, Congresswoman Gabriella Calloway in Libby's party, is seeking a private interview with Aiden."

"That's because she's heard the rumors that he's been asked to run as the opposition's candidate against Libby—or Lee, if POTUS hasn't recovered fully," Jack points out. "And should Aiden decide to run, he certainly won't be financially supporting Libby and Lee's campaign."

"The Spencers also have enough money to torpedo it," I add.

"Dominic, as Aiden's private concierge, you'll call with the suggestion that she meet with you in his stead, to, er, hammer out the details," Marcus suggests. "Since the Clement Hotel is in her congressional district. Offer to meet her there. We'll reserve an adjacent room and plant eyes and ears on it. That way, should anything go wrong, Jack, Donna, and I will be close by."

It doesn't take a special decoder ring to interpret the emotions playing out on Dominic's handsome square-jawed mien. Despite supposedly being smitten with two lovely ladies, he's not opposed to a side dish every now and again—

Especially if the liaison is government sanctioned.

"I'll reach out to her immediately." Despite the nonchalance in Dominic's tone, his smirk speaks volumes.

"And because Spencer has been playing hard to get, we anticipate Gabriella will be open to compromising Dominic, if only to get even closer to Aiden," Ryan reasons. "Dominic, you'll assure her that she'll meet Aiden at the Spencer's Palo Alto estate at a time you know Ruby will be out of the house. Let's see how far Gabriella will go to convince Aiden not to run."

"If she brings up the video of 'Ruby' with Lee, we'll know Wilbur shared it with her." Even as he says this, Jack rolls his eyes.

I glance away so that he doesn't see my blush. I can't wait for Acme to find and destroy it. No doubt Lee feels that way, too.

Which reminds me: "We should put that on Mad Hacker's honey-do list: seek and destroy the video."

"Will do," Emma replies. "Once Jack realized Wilbur was holding Donna, Mad Hacker pierced his property's electronic shield. This has allowed Acme ComInt to decipher Wilbur's communication code with Russia."

"Great work on her part." Ryan replies. "As far as Gabriella is concerned: even if her liaison with Dominic clears her as a Russian asset, she still holds an ace up her sleeve. Let's not forget that she may also have a copy of Wilbur's blackmail video of Lee with Ruby. She'll use it to influence his support on any bills she wants passed."

"She'll also use it against Ruby to tap the Spencers for contributions to her party."

"Or, better yet, to force Ruby to convince 'Aiden' not to run as the opposition Party's presidential candidate." I laugh. "And I'll gladly oblige."

"How do we know that Wilbur didn't already tell Gabriella that Donna and Ruby are one and the same?" Jack asks.

"All intercepted communiques indicate he never got around to it," Emma informs us. "If you remember, Gabriella was at the Spencers' second soirée, which was solely for members of Libby's party and their donors, including Wilbur."

"Since we already suspected she was compromised, we analyzed the two mobiles in her possession," Arnie adds. "One was U.S. Government-issued, to be used for Congressional texts and emails with her aides, her political party contacts, POTUS, and of course Wilbur. The other mobile contained coded messages. We're in the process of analyzing those now. But once we knew of Wilbur's treason, as a precaution we monitored Gabriella's secret mobile of any communication between them. Thus far, we haven't seen any communiques that demonstrate that she's Russia's asset, or that of any other country. For that matter, she may use it solely to communicate with some corporate donor who has her on a short leash."

Ryan sighs. "Sadly, those arrangements are all too common."

"Good work, Acme. This plan should be a sound one," Marcus declares. "Godspeed."

Dominic, anxious to get started, can't run out of the room quickly enough—

Only to trip over Jack's quickly extended leg. "Don't forget, Lothario, you're to make the call from here: in the SKIF."

"Yes, yes, of course!" Dominic straightens his tie. "Not to worry! Bob's your uncle."

And off he goes.

As ANTICIPATED, Gabriella is tickled pink to get Dominic's call. She readily agrees to the meeting.

"I must warn you, though, madam. Master Spencer is still enticed with the offer extended to him by your opposition. However..." He allows the word to linger; to be open to suggestion.

"Yes, Mr. Fleming? Please—feel free to be *blunt*." Her last word is delivered in an enticing whisper. "In fact, I *insist* on it."

"In that case, I certainly will." The way in which he massages each word invites her to imagine the possibilities.

"Give me a break," Jack mutters.

Dominic shoots him a salute—two-fingered and backward.

From his hospital room, Arnie murmurs, "It's like watching a Bruce Lee classic! A master at his peak!"

Jack pretends to gag.

Ryan hisses, "Craig—final warning!"

At that point, even I feel the need to punch Jack's arm to shut him up.

He stifles a yelp, but nods meekly.

"I was personally titillated by your appeal to Master Spencer. Alas, my hopes were also dashed at his refusal to see the *beauty* of you... that is *your truth—nakedly exposed* to him... metaphorically speaking, that is."

"And so *much more*." Her husky murmur is a promise as well as a boast.

"Then I shall make it my duty—nay, my *mission*—that he truly believes your *heart*—amongst your oh so obvious other lovely *muscles*—is in the right place when it comes to his position." Dominic drops his voice an octave—"of which there are *many*, Gabriella." He lets that sink in.

From her gasp, I assume it has.

"Pardon, madam! I had no right to address you in such an *intimate* manner..." His pause leaves that ball exposed—metaphorically speaking, both—for her to refute.

"Oh, please! Yes! Feel free to...to be as intimate as you wish. I insist on it!"

Yes! Yes! Yes!

My applause may be silent, but my cartwheel makes the point.

"If that is the case, perhaps a clandestine rendezvous to *pound out* any *sticky wickets* is on order. I vow, milady, I will make it worth *every minute*. Nay, every *hour*."

Apparently bored by Gabriella's cooing and gushing, Dominic holds the phone away from his ear. Though this is the height of pomposity, Jack high-fives him. As he plops down beside me, he mutters, "Better him than me."

No argument there.

———

DOMINIC HAS a page-long list of items to be delivered to the suite where he is to woo Gabriella.

As Ryan peruses it, his snorts give way to grumbles and then to outright growls. Finally, with a flourish, he pulls out his lighter and sets it on fire.

Undeterred, Dominic pulls out another copy. "All... *or nothing*."

Ryan smirks, "I choose Door Number Two."

Dominic gawks. "Well! At least you'll agree to Items 1 through 17... and perhaps 35 and 44—"

"Roses, champagne, bubble bath... a furry throw rug? *Really?*" Ryan rolls his eyes. "And what the hell is *Oud Isfahan?*"

"Nothing much..." Dominic's dismissal comes with a few flicks of his finger.

Ryan's stink-eye signals he isn't impressed.

Dominic sighs. "It's an aphrodisiac. Comes in a spray bottle. It ranks very high in the pheromone Richter scale—"

At over two hundred dollars for a *teeny-weeny bottle...*

I open my mouth to point this out, but Jack slaps a hand over it. "Let's see where this goes," he whispers.

"I don't need a statistical analysis." Ryan sighs. "Those items, no more. Agreed?"

Dominic sits silently. In time, he proffers, "Agreed."

Ryan adds, "And the next time you invite me to one of your scintillating canapés and cocktail parties, I don't want to find that furry rug on your bed. *Capeeshe?*"

"Your fluency in Italian is admirable." Dominic shrugs. "*Capeeshe.*"

Ryan walks out, which is why he's not around to see Dominic fist the air.

Jack taps his shoulder. "Nice touch, the Old Ispahan. Don't you think, Donna?"

"For sure." I cluck my tongue. "But... it's so expensive!"

"No issues. Dominic has always been a 'what's mine is yours' kind of guy." Jack pauses, as if lost in thought. "Hey, Dom, did you know that Donna's birthday is coming up? I'm sure it'll make a wonderful present—after your great event, I mean."

So that Dominic gets the message loud and clear, I add, "Indubitably!"

"It's always two against one with you Craigs," he grumbles.

"No need to be jealous, Dom. Aspire for better." I hold out one hand—"Jody"—and then the other—"Teddy. Take your pick."

"You've got to hand it to Dominic. He can make a silk purse into a solid gold valise," Jack admits.

I tease, "Is that grudging respect I hear?"

"It'll probably be the only time, but yes. I mean, look at this place!"

Jack is right. The ambiance is all it should be, and much more: sweet, inviting, tantalizing. Not only are there roses in vases throughout the room, but they are also strewn on the bedspread.

"Places, folks!" Ryan growls into our earbuds. "Elvis has entered the building."

Jack and I duck into the suite across from Dominic's.

Ryan nods for us to grab the love seat that fronts the monitor showing Dominic's suite. From another screen, separate video feeds show Emma, Arnie, and Abu, all who wave at us from their various locations. I flinch at the casts sported by sidelined team members. Their assaults could have easily been deadlier. As long as the Doomsday device is still out there, Dominic, Jack and I are also at risk.

Dominic is dressed in a bespoke suit.

"That tie is a bit sloppy," Jack points out.

I take a closer look. Our associate's tie is loosened, and the top button of his shirt is undone. "No, it's a bit sexy."

Jack snickers. "I'll remember that."

I turn his way. "It wouldn't hurt to take notes."

He frowns. "I'll also remember you said that."

The doorbell rings. Dominic opens the door, then takes a step back.

Gabriella walks in. Her hand goes down and cups him until he grunts and flinches.

"Talk about taking command!" Jack declares.

She leads Dominic into the room, but she doesn't let go. He's walking backward until he topples onto the bed. By the way she tears at his clothes, she's not looking for quid pro quo. She proves it by tossing his tie on the floor, ripping off his shirt, and yanking his pants to his ankles. She then pulls his belt from them. In a few seconds, she has his hands bound and tied, and she's straddling him.

"I take it she wore nothing under her dress," Jack muses.

"Par for the course." I lean closer to the screen. "Her technique is interesting. It's like watching one of those oil wells at work."

"Only it's not crude she's sucking," Jack points out.

"Oh, hon, you are so wrong," I chide. "She's crude, alright. That ain't no streetwalker's back-alley pump and dump. It's Grade-A Primo Kegel crunching. It'll be a whole week before he's able to walk straight up again!"

Just then, Dominic lets loose with a mortifying groan that verifies my prediction.

Gabriella wastes no time in disengaging.

I wonder, "Do you think Dominic will ask if it was as good for her as it was for him?"

Jack finds this funny enough to hold his sides because he's laughing so hard. When he can speak again, he sputters, "I was just thinking the same thing!"

As Gabriella steps into heels and adjusts her skirt, she barks, "Tomorrow I'll be in San Francisco. I've got donor meetings lined up all day at the St. Francis. I should be done by six. Tell your boss to wait for me in the bar, and to be prompt. Ciao."

By now, Dominic has rolled off the bed, but he's in pain.

She stares down at him, then rolls her eyes. "Don't bother to get the door. I'll see myself out."

After she's gone, Ryan says, "Well, that went well."

My jaw drops. "You're being sarcastic, right? If she were to judge Aiden by Dominic's, er, 'performance,' I'd agree with you. But obviously she wasn't. Otherwise, we'd have to think of some other way."

"No shit!" Jack exclaims.

"Instead, she's sending a different message," I continue. "She's wants Aiden to anticipate the challenge of keeping up with her."

"I'll do my best to slow roll it. You know... not be a Dominic," Jack vows.

I wince. "If you're coining a new phrase, please don't use it in front of him. He's devastated as is."

Jack crosses his heart. "Mum's the word."

The last thing I need is for Dominic to lose confidence in his prowess. If so, Jack would be expected to pick up the slack.

Ain't happening.

A GENTLE HUM wakes me in the middle of the night. What could it be?

Then I remember the white pager given to me by the Mad Hacker. I pull it out from under my pillow. Through bleary-eyes, I read:

...wise little Alice was not going to do THAT in a hurry..

***...she had forgotten the little golden** key...*
...a great crash, as if a dish or kettle had been** broken **to pieces...
...did you ever see such a thing as a dra*wing* **of a muchness?**

Certain words or letters look different. For example, *wise* is not bold. Nor are the words "key" and "broken" or the last for letters in "drawing"...

Ah, yes—I told Mad Hacker about Carol's mailbox at the Watergate! She's letting me know that she has the roster of Broken Wing members.

She will personally leave the intel in our dear friend's mailbox. But because she's worried it may be intercepted if express-mailed, she's asking for the mailbox key so that she may put it there herself.

With so many lives at risk, she trusts no one.

Gently, I disentangle myself from Jack so that I can open the clasp on the chain around my neck. From it, I take the mailbox key.

The chain also holds the locket containing a photo of my children. Years ago, the other side held one of Carl. It has long been replaced by a photo of Jack.

Carl felt the locket was the safest place to hide a microdot with precious intel he'd stolen: lists of all of Acme's operatives and assets. He was going to hand it off to the highest bidder.

As with Carl, treason was Aiden's siren call.

Having found this list of traitors, Mad Hacker can now focus on deactivating the Doomsday device.

The sooner the better, so we can all go home.

Slowly and quietly, I rise from the bed and walk to the library. Once inside, I slip the mailbox key into *Alice's Adventures in Wonderland,* and then I pull the book, ever so slightly, so that it protrudes from its place on the shelf. That way, the Mad Hacker will know I received her message.

As I ease myself back onto the bed, Jack mumbles something. I freeze. When I hear his gentle snore, I snuggle against him again.

Instinctively, he puts his arm around me.

The thought of what awaits us is the stuff of bad dreams. Still, I force myself to sleep.

To finish this mission, I'll need all I can get.

Chapter 18

Persona

Persona is a role that someone adopts as an effort at imitation. In AI, personas help simulate more natural human conversations by allowing models to adopt different speaking styles and personalities. However, AI personas are superficial and not true emotional intelligence.

It's the only advantage humans have on this new Frankenstein. Man the pitchforks 'cause it's a comin', by golly!

JACK HAS LEFT for his meeting with Gabriella in San Francisco. Besides being armed with his God-given charm, he has strapped his Sig Sauer to his ankle holster. He also carries a syringe filled with Acme Kickapoo Joy Juice. While she's knocked out, he'll scan her mobiles for proof that she is in communication with Russia. If he's able to verify that she is indeed a mole and I hear she's fallen out a very high window, I'm fine with that.

He left a half hour ago. Though it's only an hour into the city during good traffic, Gabriella scheduled the meeting at the peak of rush hour. According to traffic reports, it should take Jack almost two hours to get there.

I hope their fuck fest is just another hour, tops. But who knows how long it'll take? She's as horny as a toad. If she likes what she sees—and feels—she may insist that he stay the night.

I'll admit it gives me the creeps to be in this monstrosity of a mansion by myself. Even Dominic finds it too spooky and went elsewhere: with Jody, to the little cottage she's rented while she's assisting us with the Spencers' events. It's a few miles away, in the old part of town, where the locals can walk to cute little shops and tons of eateries.

But the Spencers wanted to be all the way out here, where there is no neighborhood, let alone neighbors, in several miles in any direction. It must be sad to be the type of person who hates others so much that their life mission is to have no contact with them at all.

I walk into the kitchen; not because I'm hungry but because it's the only room that doesn't make me feel as if someone is looking over my shoulder. Perhaps that's because it is the epitome of comfort and warmth, esthetically and familiarly. By that, I mean there is a lot about it that reminds me of our home in Hilldale...

Wait a minute...

I stop in the middle of the room. And then I see it:

I'm standing in my kitchen at home.

I'm mean, sure, I'm really in the Spencers' kitchen. But

it's an exacting facsimile. Though its surfaces use different materials—tile versus marble countertops; laminate cabinets versus solid wood—the color scheme is identical, as is its floor plan. For example, the stove's proximity to the refrigerator and the dishwasher—

To the inch.

The kitchen table is exactly where mine would be too. And though my kitchen encompasses a great room, this one opens onto an enclosed patio. But its furniture is laid out the same as mine at home.

Except that there are no family photos anywhere.

Why hadn't I noticed this before?

There's only one thing missing: a knife from the butcher block that holds a set of twelve.

And then I see her in the shiny mirror surface of the oven:

Gabriella.

"I was wondering how long it would take you to notice." Her voice jolts me out of the shock of this surreal setting.

I turn to her. She holds the missing knife in her hand.

"What are you doing here?" I look around. "Where is Aiden?"

She snorts. "Don't you mean Jack?"

Her response stuns me into silence.

"I'm disappointed that you aren't gliding through the Pacific in a sub, on your way to our Supreme Leader."

"Let me guess: Like Wilbur, you're a Russian asset."

She nods. "To be precise, I recruited that dirty old man. He made the perfect asset: no morals, no fear. That he was driven by money and rage and all he was denied as a hungry little boy raised in a backwoods 'holler' as he used to say made him the perfect asset." She tilts her head, assessing me. "He hasn't responded to my last few pager messages, so I assume he's dead."

But of course, they'd be communicating that way, which is why Acme didn't intercept their messages.

I opine, "Yep, them's the breaks."

Gabriella sighs. "What a shame, but so true. Especially with those who aspire to sabotage your American Congress, where every politician is some pathetic version of a Wilbur Lassiter. What made him unique was that he couldn't care less who he mortified—or, for that matter, screwed over. But I'm preaching to the choir, aren't I? You knew this too." She rubs her index finger against the knife, and pouts when it pierces her skin. Imagine how surprised he was to learn who you really were! Of course, we knew we'd find out eventually."

"How? It's not like you'd ever met Ruby Spencer," I retort.

Gabriella's coarse, cruel laugh rings through the room. "Of course I hadn't! *That's because no one has, you stupid little fool!*" She scolds me with the bloodied finger. "Your audacity for even trying to pretend was what made identifying you such a delicious game." Gabriella grasps the knife in her fist. "You should have seen Wilbur's face when he learned you weren't Ruby after all, but the renowned Donna Stone Craig. I must say, I enjoyed watching him humiliate you. Especially when you realized you were eating the whore he kept on call."

To keep her talking as opposed to throwing that knife my way, I ask, "Why the head game with the lookalike kitchen? Was it supposed to scare me?"

"No—but this is." The knife flies at me.

Instinctively, I grab the thick cutting board from the kitchen counter and hold it up to shield me. The board is wide and thick enough that the knife pierces it but doesn't break it.

I flip it over so that the knife's handle allows me to use the board as a shield as I run straight at Gabriella.

By now, she's holding a Sig Sauer P365, which she aims and shoots at me.

Where the hell did that come from?

No time to ruminate. Instead, I run at her so quickly that her instinct is to make the board her target, not the parts of me that are exposed.

I don't stop when I reach her. Instead, I plow right into her, slamming her into the wall.

When we fall to the floor, the gun flies out of her hands. We both scramble for it. I grab it first, but she bites my leg. Yes, I scream out in pain, but I don't let go of the gun. Instead, my kick to her face is hard enough that it knocks her backward into a china cabinet. She curses but is cognizant enough to duck so that my bullet shatters a stack of teacups. She reaches under the cabinet and pulls out something:

Another Sig P365.

What the...

"Where the hell did that come from?" I ask.

Her cackle is vicious. "You still haven't figured it out, have you?"

"I don't know what you're talking about!"

"And now you never will." She shoots at me.

Just in time, I duck behind the counter.

The barrage of bullets shatters the glass cabinets above it, and its china and glassware.

She stops to see if I show myself. When I don't, she comes toward me. There is so much broken bric-a-brac on the floor that I can gauge her proximity. When she realizes this too, she mutters, "*Pizdets!*"

Realizing she's fucked up, I must stifle a giggle.

Though her slow steps come closer, each one gives her away—

Even when she's just a foot from me.

She doesn't know it because I'm under the counter's barstool bump out—

But she feels it when I stab her thigh with the knife.

In any language, her scream is unintelligible. When I hear the local coyotes how their sympathy, I know it's time to take off.

I jolt away, turning into the closest hallway. Bullets spray the wall behind me.

Still, I have two advantages: speed, and a mansion filled with doors and windows.

If I'm lucky, she'll bleed out before she finds me.

Since I don't know how long it will take her to reach me, what with having to drag her leg behind her, I head for the living room. Better I chance going out the front door than stay inside.

I expected the door to be locked and bolted. What I didn't expect is that I burn my fingers when I touch them.

WHAT THE HELL?

I run down a different hall: one that I know also leads to the outside grounds. But when I touch the knob to the exit door, I'm burned again.

How and why is this happening?

I need to get out of this house....

I listen for sounds of Gabriella: nothing.

I chance a look down the hall—

And a bullet flies past my head.

She has me trapped—

Except for the elevator across from this doorway. If I take it upstairs, I'll be in the master bedroom. But if I take it down, I can go out the fire exit and onto the grounds. From there, I'll run the six miles to the gate.

With each step, Gabriella groans with pain. If the elevator is already on this floor, it will open instantly. If not, she'll shoot me while I wait for it to close.

If I don't try, I die anyway.

I leap toward the elevator, pounding the button.

In an instant, it opens.

As I smack the DOWN button, a barrage of bullets whiz by, slamming into the elevator's back wall.

Better it than me.

The elevator is moving—

But it's going up.

No matter how hard I hit the button marked DOWN, it stays on its upward trajectory.

There's nothing I can do but count my lucky stars that Gabriella can't move more quickly than me. And with her injury, she'll need the elevator to get up here.

Perhaps I can stall it.

I touch the elevator's Emergency Stop button only to have it scorch my fingertip, dammit.

How long will it take it to go back down to retrieve her and bring her back to me—a minute, maybe too?

Not long enough.

I RUN THROUGH EVERY ROOM. When I get to the master bedroom, my heart flies into my throat when I see a figure:

Eight, really—

And they're all me.

I'm in Ruby's octagonal dressing room. Every wall is a full-length mirror.

It's beside the master bathroom—

Which gives me a great idea.

I go into the bathroom and open all the taps but close all the stoppers: in the shower, stand-alone tub, and dual sinks.

Next, I run to the closet and squeeze into Ruby's hot pink knee-high rubber rain boots and its matching raincoat and rain hat.

Afterward, I center the three-foot-round wooden platform already in the middle of the room. By standing upon it, Ruby can scrutinize herself in every mirror and at every angle for any flaws in herself or her attire.

Now I head to the bathroom. After donning the pair of yellow kitchen gloves used for the bathroom's clean-up, I open the drawer containing all of Ruby's roller pins and hair pins. Grabbing their baskets, I walk from the bathroom and into the dressing room, all the while strewing them, willy-nilly, on the floor. I also open Ruby's vault of jewelry, tossing its contents throughout both rooms.

And then I grab the perfume bottle of *Oud Isfahan* that I took from Dominic.

My final act is to plug the hairdryer into one of the bathroom outlets and the electric hair straightener in another. Their electrical cords are long enough that they can be placed on the floor, which is now very wet. Having already drenched the bathroom floor, the water inches through every corner of the dressing room too.

As I run to the footstool, the carpet squishes with soppy dampness.

I count down the minutes before Gabriella gets here. I don't know if my plan will work, but since I'm locked in, I'm a sitting duck to her bullets.

Which Donna will she shoot? Hopefully, not the real one.

If my plan works, she won't get off a single shot before death becomes her.

I DON'T HAVE to wait long. Even in pain, she finds the energy to chant, "Come out, come out, wherever you are, darling Donna..."

I won't answer.

Right now, the dressing room's water level is an eighth of an inch high against Ruby's dressing platform.

My eyes are trained on the dressing room door. The hand holding the perfume bottle is hidden behind me.

Finally, I hear Gabriella's slow lumber. She's now in the bedroom.

But silence comes yet again…

I look down at the water level. It's now a quarter inch high.

In time, I hear that soft gasp the comes with each of Gabriella's pained measured steps. But then it stops when she reaches the dressing room door.

I look down to gauge the water's depth: a half inch.

That will do.

I let loose with a tiny sneeze.

When she flings open the door, she's met with a miniature tsunami: just a few inches, but enough to soak her to her ankles.

Stupefied, she doesn't take her shot. Instead, she stares down, she curses loudly. This time she calls me "*blyad!*"

"A whore? Come on, Gabriella, you can do better than that," I taunt.

Hearing my voice, she looks up. She wants to say something, but she can't.

Not with the electrical shock charging through her.

Gabriella falls to the floor. The water, still trying to find its level, flows around her. Gabriella's lips tremble, but words can no longer be formed.

Not when the body is in shock.

Not while the brain is shutting down.

Carefully, I get off my perch. I only have a few seconds to say my piece:

"Here's a little gift from Dominic." I toss the perfume bottle at her.

It smacks her right between the eyes.

Not that it matters. My timing is off. She's already dead.

I take back the bottle because, hey, Dominic promised it to me.

Instead, he can present it to Jody. Brownie points.

I HEAR SOMETHING...

The jangle of a phone.

This house has a landline? Where? On what floor? I run through the house, following its ring.

It's coming from the stairwell that leads to the tunnel that exits beside the waterfall! Was it something Mad Hacker jerry-rigged?

There's only one way to find out: answer it.

Chapter 19

Catastrophe

A catastrophe is a violent incident that occurs suddenly and wreaks havoc in its wake.

We've all had an event or two that we've described as a catastrophe. But let's face it: breaking a heel before a date or getting caught in a thunderstorm without an umbrella before a job interview ain't one. Even forgetting it's your turn for school carpool does not a catastrophe make.

On the other hand, should you find yourself caught in an avalanche or swept up in a tornado, consider yourself the queen of the catastrophe one-upmanship game.

Never forget: the biggest honor isn't the bragging rights, but that you lived to tell about it.

"Thank goodness you picked up!" I'm hearing Emma's voice.

I ask, "Is this a landline?"

"You betcha!" Emma replies. "Let's pray this old school telephone company stuff never goes away."

"Why is it live? And for that matter, how did you get the number?" I wonder.

"Arnie had the smart idea to check the house's building permits at the county planning department," Emma explains. "Not only did he find this creepy monster mansion's floor plan, he also discovered that the house's original construction contractor was upset because the estate was a telecommunication dead zone. The guy could never reach his crew via cell service, so he had a landline installed. Lucky for us, he's still under contract for the house's ongoing maintenance."

"I'll say!" I exclaim.

"But Donna... You should brace yourself for...for what I have to tell you." I've never heard such dread in Ryan's voice.

Please, God, please! Don't let it be about the man I love with all my heart... "Just... Tell me, Ryan."

He sighs. Then: "The whole thing was faked."

"Come again?" I ask not because I didn't hear him but because I just don't understand why he'd say that.

"The plane crash never happened," he says. "*It was faked.*"

"But..." In my mind, I retrace the timeline of my knowledge of the Spencers. "How do you know this? You said so yourself: it'll be several months before rescue workers can get to the wreckage to verify if there were survivors—"

"We now know there is no need for them to go because *no plane crashed*—let alone with the Spencers on board," he insists. "Donna, let me start at the beginning—"

"Yes, please, Ryan! I'm so confused!" Not to mention angry. And scared.

Was all of this for nothing? How could that be?

"The only reason the Federal Aviation Administration informed Marcus of the crash in the first place was because the Spencers were Americans of some renown," Ryan explains. "But after Wilbur Lassiter was proven to be a spy—and with all the strange occurrences at the Spencers' homes—Marcus asked Carol's division, the NCC, to go over every communique referencing the flight. The analysis was just finalized. One of the communiques was a manifest from the U.S. Customs and Border Protection. It's the governmental entity that approves all private aircraft that arrive or depart from a foreign port. As it turns out, the document the FCC received was faked. The Spencers' plane never left Davos because... Well, because it was never there to begin with."

Guffawing, I declare, "I assume that next you'll tell me that Aiden isn't dead after all."

"You're right. Aiden isn't," Ryan says.

"I was joking! I hope you are too." A cold chill runs through me. "Do you mean to say Aiden and Ruby are alive?"

"Not in the way you think"—he hesitates—"because the Spencers *don't exist.*"

"But... How can that be?" I ask. "Everyone knew them! At least, those who worked in the tech field."

"You're wrong, Donna," Ryan insists. "Everyone knew *of* them, as Acme knows all too well. But no one has ever *met* them. It's why we were able to plant you and Jack as their stand-ins."

"But...you've got to admit that it's ludicrous—I mean,

them *not* existing!" I exclaim. "You're describing... Well, I guess you'd call it a *live* deepfake! And that doesn't make any sense at all!"

"Which brings us back to all the strange happenings taking place there, in that house, including the attempt to kill Arnie and Abu." Ryan takes a deep breath: "Donna, Aiden is not 'he,' but 'it.' And 'it' is the house!"

The house? "How could that be?" I ask.

"According to Emma, Mad Hacker suspected something was not right about their houses, so she did some digging on how and why," Arnie adds. "Two of her dark web sources mentioned rumors about a Russian AI project that somehow got out of control."

"I'll say! This house... It has a mind of its own!" I think of all I've been through in this monster mansion.

Suddenly it feels deadly cold in here.

"The name 'AIDEN' is an acronym," Ryan continues. "It stands for 'Artificial Intelligence Doomsday Explosion Nanobot'."

"How do you know this?" I ask.

"While Mad Hacker was on the grounds of the Spencer's Palo Alto mansion, she stumbled across three bodies," Ryan explains. "The dead men were members of a five-person FSB tech ops team who came to the U.S. via a submarine that surfaced off the coast of Santa Clara County, also near the island where Wilbur was told by his FSB handlers to rendezvous with you."

"It's a small world after all," I'm joking.

"Apparently not," Ryan replies.

Why do my jokes go over his head?

"Their mission was to live in the house, undetected by the CIA or FBI," Arnie adds.

"Why build AIDEN here, on the territory of their largest enemy?" I wonder aloud.

"Frankly, it was a stroke of genius," Ryan declares. "Just think about it! Silicon Valley is the heart and soul of our country's largest technology brain trust: the tech companies and the universities that serve them. The house's proximity is ideal for covert hacking. For example, the FSB team laid malicious USB cables that diverted tech company intel. It also used LAN turtles, OMG plugs, and systematic passive logging to scrape the intellectual property of the tech firms that work with the U.S. Government, security firms, financial institutions, and social media companies worldwide."

"In other words, housing AIDEN in the heart of Silicon Valley paid off big time," I point out.

"Sadly, yes," Ryan concedes. "But then the house started its shenanigans. For example, it blocked communiques to and from each other, and from their Moscow handlers."

"There were several times it did the same to us," I reply. "Like that time Broderick told me he'd reached out to 'Aiden' and got no reply. It played us as if we were pieces on a chess board."

"If AIDEN felt threatened, it would turn off the fans so that the servers would overheat," Ryan continues. "On two different incidents, the FSB techs who went into the bowels of the house to restart them were fatally electrocuted."

"Like Arnie and me!" Abu exclaims.

"Except you lived to tell the tale," I remind him.

"The three surviving FSB operatives sent distress signals to their handlers, requesting to abort the mission," Ryan explains. "They thought it had been received and that a sub was on its way to retrieve them. Instead, they never made it out of the compound."

"What happened to them?" I ask.

"AIDEN's compound is guarded by robotic artillery—essentially, sniper rifles hidden high in the trees," Arnie replies. "The surviving operatives decided to take the chance that they could avoid it. Instead, they were gunned down when they stepped on sensors that signaled their locations."

The guns in the woods will try to take me out too.

"Donna, bottom line: AIDEN has far exceeded the FSB's ability to keep it contained," Ryan concludes.

"And we—that is, Acme—aided and abetted AIDEN's worldwide infiltration," I deduce. "Our mission allowed it to scrape intel from every device we scanned: not just those of the tech industry bigwigs who came to our shindigs, but the devices of both political parties' politicians and their largest donors."

"By now, AIDEN will have infiltrated their personal data, perhaps those of their personal contacts, too."

"Correct. To my utmost shame, Acme opened all the floodgates." Ryan's voice trembles with this admission. "It could take the United States years, perhaps decades, to reclaim its standing in the technology front. Its soft power won't be trusted, either. In the meantime, Russia's threat to enact identical operations in other democracies would be reason enough for those countries to kowtow to its economic demands, not to mention its political ones. No need to plant doubt in the minds of its populace with social media deep-fakes when its biggest fear is being physically blown off the map."

"But Russia no longer controls AIDEN," I point out. "Like all AI, it's yet to be regulated. AIDEN is free to kill off each country one by one."

"And so cleanly, too," Emma adds. "Why allow humankind to kill itself polluting the air and water with radiation when it can simply turn our nations into an autocratic slave state under one master?"

"Vlad must think it will still need a 'face," Ryan deduces. "So, why not his?"

"Now that we know the server farm in the house's basement are what drives the doomsday device, I need to disarm it," I declare.

"No, Donna, you need to get out of there—like, *yesterday!*" Arnie insists.

"Even Mad Hacker has been trying to reach you," Emma explains. "She said if we get to you first, to tell you, '*Always speak the truth, think before you speak, and write it down afterwards.'*"

It's Mad Hacker's way of warning me to keep the pager at hand so that she can communicate with me—

And guide me out of this six-square-acre nightmare.

"I can't leave until I disarm AIDEN," I argue.

"Don't you get it?" Arnie retorts. "The whole time you've been there, it's been studying you; reading your mind, as it were. AIDEN knows how you think! It will anticipate your instincts and responses."

"Good to know." My voice is barely a whisper. "Then this is goodbye—for now. In the meantime, get ahold of Jack. *Tell him not to come back here!*"

I hang up.

And I go back upstairs.

I'll give it what it wants: a chance to kill me.

Instead, I'll kill AIDEN.

PENNIES. All I need is just a few pennies.

Today, it costs three and a half cents to mint a single Copper Abe. And now that we've moved to digital currency, soon coins—copper, nickel, not to mention paper bills—will be a thing of the past.

I go to my purse and pray that I find some. Even a few will do...

Yep, I have seven pennies. It's not enough, but it's better than nothing.

After pocketing them, I put on the rubber cleaning gloves and head for the kitchen: specifically, its ceiling fixture. Taking a foot ladder, I unscrew the fixture and then its bulb, which I replace with a penny. I screw the bulb back into place, and then I flick on the light. A faint pop tells me what I need to know: its breaker is incapacitated.

But when I test the kitchen door that leads to the backyard, I find it locked. So are the kitchen windows. I walk through the downstairs. Not-one of the windows can be opened. The same is true about the exterior doors. Apparently, they are on a different circuit breaker. Maybe on several different ones.

To get out of here, I'll have to figure out which breakers controls at least one exit out of this house of horrors.

I head for the stairs leading to AIDEN's server farm. As if reading my mind, the walls shake. It feels like an earthquake is rocking the house. When I reach the room's door, its knob scalds me through the gloves, but I don't let go. Instead, I lean on the door with all my might. It's enough force to create a slim opening between the door and its lock. When I slip in a penny, the current is broken.

I open it:

The room is much larger than I imagined. It's width and depth run the full length of the house. Where do I start? I must make up my mind quickly. Otherwise, I'll faint from the heat. This time, I opt to short out an electrical socket: specifically, a multi socket against a far wall. As I run over, the servers get louder and louder, hurting my ears.

I won't—*I cannot*—let AIDEN stop me.

When I reach the multi-socket, I pull out just one that is connected to a server. I don't pull out all the pennies at once, but just one, placing it against the socket before putting the plug back. Sparks fly off one of the machines. It groans angrily, as if it's spewing cruel curses—

But then it dies.

I do the same routine with another socket: pull out the plug, put a penny against the socket, reattach the plug—

And watch as sparks fly while the server dies, all the while growling ferociously until it sizzles out.

I repeat this routine again; and yet again, until I'm out of pennies.

But the house wants to show me who's boss. The room is now the temperature of an oven. I run quickly to the door. Instinctively, I leave it open. Bad move: the hot air follows me up the steep steps. When I get to the top of the stairwell, I touch the doorknob with one of my rubber gloves. It's so hot that the glove melts at its touch. I yelp when the heat meets my palm, and I bite my tongue so that I don't scream in pain as I fly into the hall.

Chapter 20

Helldoomed

If someone assumes that their fate is to end up in Hell, they believe they are helldoomed.

It's best to keep such assumptions in perspective. For example:

• Being stuck on a highway for several hours even if you haven't moved but one or two exits does not make you helldoomed.

• Catching your best friend and your hubby in flagrante delicto does not mean you're helldoomed—but he and his ho tart sure as hell are.

• And finally, you're not helldoomed if you get caught having an affair. However, alimony may be in order, which is quasi-helldoom, depending on how badly your divorce attorney handles things.

—————

It's time to get out of this house.

To my dismay, none of the blown fuses controlled an exit. The exterior doors and windows either shock or burn me.

I'm doomed to die in this house of horrors.

A thought occurs to me: perhaps the electrical charge that flowed through the bedroom shorted its digital controls.

I go back into the bedroom to test my theory. I'm right! The window opens easily.

AIDEN will be tracking me through my body heat, which will trigger the robotic artillery. Knowing this, I'll need a Substitute Donna.

I look around—

And there she is: Gabriella.

Though her body is cold, she'll be my shield against AIDEN's artillery.

But first, I must make her look like me. At the same time, I must make myself invisible to AIDEN'S facial recognition software.

I take off what I'm currently wearing—the hot pink rain gear—and put it on her. I do the same with Ruby's red-haired wig.

To create my FRS invisibility shield, I strip down, opting for all-white: pants, and a turtleneck sweater. I pull my hair back and cover it with a white scarf, starting at my forehead. I have a jar of white clay that is supposed to be a face mois-turizer. It will be my kabuki mask. I slather on the stuff. But since I can't cover my eyes, I roam through the accessories the Jody pulled for Ruby until I find a pair of mylar sunglasses.

The further I am from AIDEN'S visual sensors, the better. Since the exterior ones will be most affected by uncontrolled elements—light, noise, and the movement of any animals on the property—it's best that I go out a window. From the third floor, it's one hell of a drop. But since it's the only one that opens, I must attempt it.

I grab the sheets off the bed and tie them end to end. I don't know if they'll hold. Even if they do, they won't reach all the way to the ground. I'll still have two more stories beneath me and a slate patio.

Gabriella must land first, and face down. That way should my sheet rope break, her body will cushion my fall.

I grab as many belts as I can find from Ruby's wardrobe and from Aiden's. With them, I'll strap Gabriella's body to mine.

After sitting down on the bed, I roll her into my lap, like a life-size puppet. I then strap her ankles to mine and belt her knees to mine. Next, I buckle two belts together so that I can weave them between our legs and up the back to our waists and buckle us together. With two more belts, I secure her under her breasts so that she flattens mine against her back.

Finally, so that her head doesn't flop forward, I wrap a belt around her neck and halter it beneath my armpits.

It takes all my strength to propel us off the bed. Just when I think I can stand up straight with her—

I topple backward, onto the bed.

Though I struggle to get up again, I am weighted down by her.

"Jesus, Donna! What the hell are you doing?" Jack's voice comes from the doorway. He runs over. When he sees Gabriella, he's stunned. "Why is she... and you..."

I crane my neck so that at least one eye sees beyond

Gabriella's head. "Long story short: first, as we deduced because of her connection with Wilbur, Gabriella was a Russian agent. Luckily, she lost in her shootout with me. Secondly, the whole house is AIDEN, which stands for 'Artificial Intelligence Doomsday Explosion Nanobot'. The house is the Doomsday device. And finally, I need to use Gabriella's body as a human shield to get out of here. Otherwise, my body heat will set off AIDEN's covert robot artillery, which is up in the trees throughout the property." I roll my eyes. "Now, answer me this: what the hell are you doing back here when I specifically told Ryan to tell you to stay away? More to the point: how the hell did you get into the house when AIDEN has it in lockdown?"

Stunned, Jack replies. "I used my front door key."

"Oh..." Hell yeah, I'm stymied. "Well then... We should leave that way as well."

"Seriously, Donna, I don't know whether to laugh or to burn this crazy joint to the ground myself."

"I vote for the latter. But not until we're far enough away that we don't get singed too." I squirm one hand out from under Gabriella and hold it out to him. "The house has—or *had* me under attack! I was able to disarm seven of AIDEN's servers. But there are at least another forty down there. Emma was supposed to contact you and tell you to stay away from here since I was about to head out anyway."

Jack kisses the burn on my palm. "I never got any of Emma's messages."

"Before you left, AIDEN must have put a lock on your phone's messaging and call mechanism."

"Makes sense." Jack frowns. "In fact, when I got to the St. Francis's bar, one of the bartenders handed me a note that said Gabriella's donor meeting was cancelled and she was back in Palo Alto. She asked to meet me here instead. I tried to call you to confirm, but your cell rolled to voice mail. I also texted you, but I got no response."

Bad sign. "That was AIDEN again. And now that he's got you here, he can take us out together."

"Nah. Not happening. The bartender also gave me this." He hands me a white pager. "Weird message, though. What do you make of it?"

He holds it out to me to read:

**Yes, but some crumbs must have got in as well,'
the Hatter grumbled...
The Knave did so, very carefully, with one foot.**

"It's from Mad Hacker! This is her way of saying that she rigged the pager so that it blocks audio, visual, and body-heat sensors. It's our only hope for dodging AIDEN's covert artillery while it guides us out of the woods."

"AIDEN thought of everything." Jack winces. "Let's hit the road. But first, dump the dead body overcoat. Besides slowing us down, it's not a pretty look."

I'd punch him if I didn't want to kiss him.

But first things first: get the hell out of here.

OUR ESCAPE from the Doomsday mansion is made in silence. From what we can tell, few critters live on its grounds or in its bushes. Few birds nest in its trees, for good reason, I imagine. If all it takes is a trill or caw to set off

AIDEN's covert artillery, they've witnessed its destruction firsthand.

The woods are not paradise. It's a helldoom.

On the upside, the pager is proving to be a spot-on sherpa. If we're within four feet of a heat sensor that will trigger a barrage of bullets from AIDEN's hidden guns, the screen writes the appropriate message to divert our route yet keep us on our path to the gate. For example, it may be something like MOVE THREE STEPS TO YOUR LEFT AND THEN GO STRAIGHT.

Since the pager's shields cover a mere five-foot radius, we move in lockstep. Nothing keeps a couple closer than a brisk arm-in arm walk. Am I right?

When we left the house, the sun was already well below the horizon. Despite Mad Hacker's assurance that the pager's shield can block AIDEN's various scanning devices, the psychological aftershocks of being in its house has kept us silent and constantly looking over our shoulders.

"The pager wants us to take five steps to the left and then keep moving forward another six, then left for three." Though I hold the pager and whisper its directives or warnings, Jack insists on taking the lead.

I nudge him in the right direction. We stay silent for the next half mile. Like me, Jack wants to run, but we quash the urge: better safe than sorry.

A half mile later, the forest levels off. The pager reads: TURN RIGHT HERE. GO EIGHT STEPS, THEN TURN LEFT.

By following its directions, we end up at a clearing: the driveway.

We're almost at the gate! Look! We can see it from here!"
I whisper.

The full moon reveals the wide wrought iron gate that is
the only way in or out of the property surrounded by a six-
foot tall brick wall.

"The pager tells us to keep parallel to the driveway, but
we should stay in the woods," Jack insists.

I nod.

Grabbing my arm, Jack starts in that direction—

But then suddenly, a dark form appears.

Shivers run up my spine. I stifle a scream, but it's too
late. Our predator comes toward us, now looming so large
that, instinctively, I duck, until I force myself to see our
attacker:

It's a large, snow-white owl on its evening hunt. The
sound of its wings, flapping wildly, reminds me of the
numerous close calls Jack too has endured these past few
days.

It swoops over our head—

Until a barrage of bullets takes it down.

One of the bullets ricochets off the brick wall—

And into me.

My stifled groan doesn't get Jack's attention because he's
mystified by the craziness that seems to have taken over the
woods. An acrid stench fills the air. Smoke scrims our vision
of the forest's flaming trees. Their sap creates the sparks that
shoot from their branches and tops like newly lit firecrackers.

Agog, Jack finally looks over at me. The shock in his eyes
turns to dread when he notices my sweater, now soaked and
shiny and brightly scarlet. Cursing silently, he jumps into
action. Yanking off his shirt, in no time he's torn it into strips

to make a tourniquet in the hope of staunching the blood flowing out of me.

"Please, God! Not now! Donna, damn it! you can't bleed out now! ..."

Try as I might, my mouth won't form the words I must say to calm his curses or answer his prayer.

My world goes black.

Chapter 21

Day of Reckoning

Eventually, the time comes when one's misdeeds must be faced. This is known as "The Day of Reckoning."

Example: all those summer months in which the Teenaged and Young Adult You sunbathed. Yes, your brown, toned skin looked beautiful then. But today, those hazy lazy sunny days are why you now curse every wrinkle, furrow, and pucker.

Let's face it: those lines on your face don't give you "character"—

Except on Halloween.

As I HOVER between life and death, my world is a kaleidoscope of memories.

I remember lights: on Christmas trees, in Halloween lanterns, and from the spark of my parent's cigarettes glowing in the pitch-black darkness of my bedroom as they looked in on me.

I remember colors: Peeps, in pinks and yellows, buried deep within the bright green shredded cellophane of my Easter basket.

And I remember the vibrant hues of every flower found at the foot of every rainbow.

In time, my memories turn to the faces of friends and family. The living, their voices peppered with their zest for life, wonder if I can hear them as they fret over my survival. The dead, now knowledgeable of The Other Side, look more at peace. Even in my State of Betweenness, one would think they'd feel cold upon touch, right? Not so! If anything, they are cozy warm, like a breeze on a mild summer day, or a cushioned rocker beside a crackling fire.

Be they from my Past, Present or Future, they whisper their love.

These happy memories bring a comfort akin to tides lapping against the shore, or the soft fur of the pet that insists you stroke it as it warms your lap; or your lover's familiar yet still intoxicating pheromones.

In this state, I also remember the feeling of pending doom. Ghosts of missions past come to taunt as much as to haunt. There is the Quorum's Eric Webber, followed by Salem Rahmin al-Sadah, whose company, Graffias International, was also a Quorum front. Because these men underestimated everything about me—my gender, my power, my drive to beat them before they ruined the world as we know it—they now curse me as they rot in the ground.

I shoo them away. They deserve no place in my subconscious. I leave them for the pesky bugs that nibble on their remains.

Lee's long-dead wife, Babette—one of the Quorum's long-embedded operatives—also stops by. She teases that I'm as pale as a ghost!

"Have you looked in the mirror lately?" I retort.

We both know the answer: she can't, because the dead don't reflect light.

Catherine "CeeCee" Martin visits too. She married Evan's father, Robert, my high school crush. She then murdered him to grab sympathy votes while she was her political party's presidential candidate. She was also Putin's pawn. Killed while in prison, her secrets died with her. Is there a special place in Hell for those who kill the innocent for personal gain? If so, it's where she resides.

Then there's the triple-agent chess master, Mason Ledbetter. He was the first Russian asset to try to present me to Putin as a gift, but obviously not the last. I knocked him into his fiery grave.

Speaking of flesh peddlers, Wilbur stops by too. Now officially a ghoul, his jack-o-lantern smile becomes him. He must read my mind because he declares, "Aw, shucks, Donna, I'll take that as a compliment!"

He's fishing, but I ain't biting. "Now, shoo," I grumble. "You'll scare away the good folk..."

Yes, they are here too:

There is my father. Timidly he touches my hand. Love flows strongly and deeply from his fingertips. I raise my lips into a smile, but the words *I love you* are stuck in my throat.

Because he can read my mind, he says, "I know, darling, I know..." As was his way, the effort to acknowledge any affection is met with embarrassment strong enough that he fades back into oblivion. He knows I won't be upset. The fact that he made the effort is all that counts.

And besides, he can't compete with the bright light that is my mother, all pearls and dimples and the sweet smell of Chanel. Mother comes bearing her signature sick-call dish: a cherry pie. She puts it within reach, but warns, "It's still warm from the oven, so give it time to cool…"

While she walks around the bed, tucking in its sheets so that it's nice and tidy again, I feel there is so much I must tell her: How Mary loves wearing her pearls, how Trisha takes after her in the kitchen, and how Jeff, now a young man of sixteen, is the spitting image of her father at the same age.

But my words come out jumbled.

Noting my frustration, she pats my hand. "I already know, sweet Donna. Because I'm always at your side."

I nod, but my eyelids are too heavy to stay open. Maybe it's for the best since she's already told me what I needed to hear:

That those souls who have passed before us are still within reach.

THERE ARE times when I hear Jack breathing.

At other times, I hear him crying.

But it's his praying that gives me the strength to inch my finger close enough to nudge his hand.

To sigh loudly enough that he hears me.

To force my eyes to open.

Seeing how he watches me, I know the pain and effort was worth it by what I see there: jubilation.

Hope.

Love.

He starts to speak, but I shake my head. "Give me a few silent moments to admire the man who has saved my life yet again."

And, so we sit here, steeped in relief and the knowledge that once again we will revel in each other's company, laugh at each other's jokes, and sway together as we dance in each other's arms.

More so, we will make the fierce passionate love that celebrates being alive yet one more day.

Rarely do we discuss our many close calls. Despite seeing each other in precarious situations—or, worse still, at death's door—we've brushed the fear away. The memory is a pesky reminder of how quickly our lives could end.

Though not our love.

But now, by the way Jack's smile flattens, I realize he's breaking our awkward tradition. This mission has made him want to face the topic we've not yet discussed: a death too quick.

One that will leave us no chance to say all that was left unspoken.

"Donna, I'm sorry you had to endure Wilbur's sadism," he begins. "I can't even imagine how you felt when you saw the submarine break the waves."

"Instead, imagine my joy at seeing you standing there." My voice shakes at the memory. "I know it wasn't easy to tell the children I'd...died."

"When I told them, I was still under the assumption you

were dead." Jack sighs. "I had them meet me in the backyard beneath their old tree house." I hear the catch in his throat. "I tried to plan my words carefully. But..." Jack's voice trails off. "Despite what we do for a living, I never thought the day would come when you'd die and leave me. Leave *us*." He stops to face me. "I was bereft. The one person in the world who gave my life meaning was no longer there to share it. I was speechless. I thought that perhaps if I wrote down what I should say and read it to them, it would be easier. Instead, the sentences died in my throat. At that point, I realized I should speak from my heart; to let the tears flow. That way, they'd know it was fine for them to cry too."

"Wilbur taunted me with a satellite feed of your eulogy at my funeral," I admit. "I'm sure it was distressing to you—and the children—to go through the motions."

"By then we'd intercepted Wilbur's message to Vlad that he had a present for him: you. Still, Acme thought it best for Wilbur to have visual proof of my grief. No better place to display it than at your memorial service."

"I'm shocked that Acme would remove the GPS block on its headquarters!"

"Not to worry, Don. The building's satellite coordinates are altered to read as if it's a hundred miles from its true location. The coordinates change daily. DARPA is testing it now for its own use."

"Another win for Acme." Despite my pain, I force myself to smile. "You know, for a second there, I imagined you winking at me."

"I figured that sadist would play it for you. If so, I hoped you'd understand that I was going to bring you home, come hell or high water." Jack's chuckle is half-hearted. "The water was high enough during your rescue, wouldn't you say?"

That horrible day. That wonderful, awful, horrible day...

My eyes threaten tears, so I look away.

"I'm—I'm so sorry, Donna! I... only meant to say—"

Now I'm crying. "Stop, please!" I command.

The color drains from Jack's face. "Of course, I didn't mean to upset you!"

"I'm not upset!" I'm blubbering now. "I'm in love—with you! All over again! For always being here for me, and protecting me, and for loving me so much..."

He stares but he doesn't move.

"Jack, are you listening? ...*If ever there was a time to kiss me, it's now!*"

So that he knows I mean business, I pull him in close and lift my face to his.

Jack's mouth moves to mine. His lips are ravenous.

My body aches for the rest of him.

At least, I think it does, until his lips moved down my neck.

And then I groan from the pain—

Until I tap my pain med line.

Ah.... *relief.*

I whisper, "Now, where were we?"

"JACK SAYS you insisted on being released yesterday. I'm surprised your surgeon agreed." We've been on the secure-line conference call for less than a minute and already Ryan is scolding me.

Thank goodness some things never change.

"And hello to you too!" I blow him a kiss, which deflates his scowl.

Is that a grin I'm seeing? I don't ask. That would be pushing my luck.

The faces of all my Acme teammates now also fill the screen. Arnie and Abu still sport bandages from their *ex machina* altercations. Emma, at Arnie's side, lovingly strokes the arm that is in a cast. Abu's cast, which runs from wrist to above the elbow on his pitching arm, doesn't let this stop him from hitting the face on an InterPol wanted poster with a tennis ball repeatedly. I take it as a sign that his tussle with AIDEN has renewed his faith in his ability to do his job. I get that. I now wonder if I'll ever hear another get-rich-quick scheme from my partner in government-sanctioned crime.

Dominic's demeanor is uncharacteristically solemn. There is no witty banter, and his usually sly smile has been replaced by a stiff upper lip. The wounds Gabriella inflicted on him aren't physical but psychic. He's living proof that pride goeth before the fall.

DNI Branham is now joining the conference," Emma warns us.

Ryan's arched brow signals his mandate: our best behavior is expected.

I shoot him a peace sign that his message has been received—

Sort of.

I take it as a good sign that Marcus is smiling. "Before Acme's recap of its mission, I have some good news to relay. President Kentfield has been released from Walter Reed. Though her injuries still require crutches and some bandages, her doctors have pronounced her fit to resume her duties."

My Acme team claps and whoops at this news.

"The American public will be happy to see her on her feet, not to mention back on the road," Arnie points out. "In fact, since the accident, her approval ratings have gone through the roof."

"Folks prefer the known to the unknown," Abu reasons. "Especially if POTUS's policies are making their lives easier."

"What did *Time* call her when it named her 'Person of the Year'? ... Oh yeah! 'America's No-Drama Queen,'" Emma adds.

Jack leans toward me and murmurs, "What do you think? Is Lee relieved or disappointed?"

"Totally relieved!" My tone is emphatic.

Perhaps too much so because it wipes the smirk off Jack's face.

Stupid me, I should let sleeping dogs lie! The last thing I need is for Jack's jealousy to rear its ugly head, and for no reason—

Okay, admittedly, the last thing Lee would ever want Jack to know is that he wasn't faking his response to our being too close for either's comfort or that nature took its course, as it were.

If Wilbur had planned to hand-deliver me to the submarine captain, having sunk into the ocean took care of that. All proof is now buried at sea with the treasonous senator.

So, no use crying over spilled...*anything.*

"As for Acme's mission to take down AIDEN, I want to applaud you for its success," Marcus continues. "AIDEN's inferno reached an intensity so great that crews from every firehouse in the state were on hand. As of yesterday, the fire has been successfully contained."

"Have the firefighters gone below ground to see if AIDEN's server farm is still standing?" I ask.

"Yes, but they had to wait until this morning when the underground access tunnels temperature had cooled off enough to allow for safe passage," Marcus explains. "It's been confirmed that not only had the server farm was decimated, but all the cable and satellite connections were also destroyed."

"Bottom line: Russia's rogue mission could not repel Acme's assault," Jack points out.

At that moment, I receive a text message:

"… the hall was very hot…
…hot buttered toast,) she very soon finished it
off."

But of course, Mad Hacker would want to listen in on the op's wrap-up.

"That doesn't mean another AIDEN won't one day be let loose on the world," Arnie mutters.

"Let's take a moment to enjoy the here and now, shall we?" Dominic pleads.

"Which brings me to Acme's commendations." Marcus nods toward Abu, and then to Arnie. "I'm quite aware that this mission incurred physical blowback to two of your team members. Ryan, because of the nature of this op, no line item is needed but do include all medical expenses in your final invoice so that Acme is duly recompensed. I suggest that you also include a month's vacation time for the injured."

Hearing this, Abu is stunned enough to forget to catch his tennis ball.

Ryan stifles a groan at its onscreen fly-by.

"Donna, you took a bullet in service to your country. For such conspicuous gallantry and intrepidity at the risk of life above and beyond the call of duty, POTUS has deemed you deserving of a Presidential Medal of Freedom. However, because of the top-secret classification of this mission, the ceremony will take place at Acme."

"Wherever it happens, I'd be honored," I assure him.

"On the topic of treason—specifically as it pertains to Senator Broderick Page, Senator Wilbur Lassiter, and Congresswoman Gabriella Calloway, an interesting item was dropped in Carol Wise's mailbox at the Watergate," Marcus divulges. "It was a list of all Broken Wing members in Congress with photos of their FSB kompromat files."

Ryan mulls that for a moment. "It came from an anonymous source?"

"Yes. However," Marcus pauses. Then: "It is POTUS's intention to delay its public knowledge—for the time being anyway. Her position is that the traitorous actions of such high-ranking elected officials is best addressed after the upcoming election."

"Sir, with all due respect: that is utter bullshit!" Jack counters. "If anything, we should hold our public officials to a higher standard. Doesn't the American public have a right to know about Russian sabotage on U.S. soil and who abetted it?"

"Trust me, POTUS has the same concerns. She has

every intention of revisiting this mandate *after* the election. The FBI's Counterterrorism division is building its legal case against them now. Its roundup will take place the day after the election."

"And now that POTUS has proof of the unleashed power of Artificial Intelligence, how will she be dealing with it?" I ask.

"You'll be relieved to know that she has already signed an executive order outlining regulations on the legality of its use, and she is demanding that Congress write legislation to support it. She will also rally the United Nations on the topic and make it a priority at the G7 Summit." He leans in. "I don't need to tell you that, should she lose the upcoming election, there's no guarantee it will be addressed *at all*."

This is his way of saying she's the world's best shot at stopping AI's annihilation of humankind.

"When the time comes, Acme offers its assistance," Ryan says.

"By the way, all copyrights and trademarks that were formerly owned by Aiden Spencer were transferred to a new legal owner," Marcus informs us.

Ryan frowns. "Are his initials VP?"

"I'm happy to report that it isn't a Russian entity. It's something call the Alice P. Liddell World Harmony Trust." Marcus replies.

I recognize the name as that of the little girl for whom Lewis Carroll wrote *Alice in Wonderland*. No need to dig deeper. Both actions have Mad Hacker's digital fingerprints all over them. More power to her. I can guess who that was, and where it was obtained: by Mad Hacker during her perusal of AIDEN's data.

"On a final note: Lee and Eve's wedding is next week. They've asked POTUS to marry them. I'm sure she'll be happy to bestow Donna's medal prior to the nuptials. Does that work for everyone?"

"Yes," I reply.

"The sooner the better," Jack mutters.

Marcus doesn't catch this, but Ryan does, and scowls.

"I look forward to seeing you all there." Marcus waves, then signs off.

"Well, that went well." Ryan proclaims.

"We'll see," Jack murmurs.

"I want to smack him, but that would hurt too much— me, not Jack.

The call was painful enough.

Chapter 22

Utopia

One definition of Utopia is "an imaginary place where ideal perfection—especially as it pertains to laws, government, and social conditions—reigns supreme."

However, others call it "an impractical scheme for social improvement."

If it's okay to believe in magic, angels, leprechauns, unicorns, and Lotto, then why not the existence of Utopia?

I rest my case.

Now that I'm home, Jeff and Trisha are kind and gentle with each other whenever I'm within hearing distance. And although Jack and I have relieved Mary and Evan of their housesitting duties with their younger siblings, they insist on lingering here.

If it's true that absence makes the heart grow fonder,

watching a loved one fight off death is the ultimate wake-up call and reason enough to show your love often.

In the mere week I've been home, our children's random acts of kindness have been ceaseless. Trisha insists on making all my favorite dishes. Jeff, formerly the messiest of my kids, has become a neat freak. And if he sees me napping on the backyard hammock, he pays the neighborhood kids to play a block over in Hilldale Park. Mary and Evan do the grocery shopping and clean up after every meal.

Jack is my constant companion. He's taken on the role of my personal sentry, never leaving my side. If we get a call from Acme, he monitors it first. Ryan has gotten the message: until my wound has healed, I'm only available for consultations.

To that end, I do post-op analyses—P.O.A.'s for short—of those Acme missions that were aborted; or worse yet, failures.

The P.O.A.'s that sustained casualties are the hardest to watch. They are sullen reminders that even with an experienced ops team, anything and everything can go wrong.

After my sixth P.O.A., Ryan calls. "Hey, um... I've got a request."

"Name it."

"Can you... If you don't mind, can you... What I'm trying to say is, the feedback on your audio P.O.A.'s is that they're sort of... well... they sound as if you're having too much fun."

Hmmmm. "What exactly do you mean?"

"To be specific, and I quote, 'the narrator's reads are much too 'playful,' 'breathy,' and—here's the response most given: '*sexy.*'"

"Question, Boss Man: do *you* find me sexy?"

"You... *personally?* Because, truth is, I find you somewhat annoying."

"No, silly goose! I mean my voice! Does it sound sexy to you?"

Ryan is silent. Too silent.

"Yo, Ry—are you still there?"

He sighs. "I could see how, if someone hadn't met you in person and been the butt of one of your jokes, let alone picked up on your sarcasm, then yeah, maybe they'd find it a bit *titillating.*" Ryan still doesn't sound totally convinced.

"Well then, you have your answer. The issue is theirs, not mine. They're projecting their own enjoyment of what we do into my read."

"We kill for a living! Under any other circumstance, we'd be considered psychopaths."

"Okay, sure, I see your point." *Yikes.* "On the other hand, by keeping things light, bright, and gay, our operatives get a contoured message that plays to Acme's advantage: 'It's okay to enjoy what we do in service of our country—but still, let's be careful out there!'"

Silence. Then: "Could work." He grunts a grudging goodbye.

I'll take it.

I'll do a few more videos but then call it quits. That way, perhaps one will be nominated for an Acmy: our annual awards ceremony honoring the best of the best for what we do. Having already won the "BEST HONEYPOT" and "ASSASSIN OF THE YEAR, it would be nice to add a "BEST TRAINING VIDEO" statuette to the collection above the fireplace.

None are worthy of being the mantle's centerpiece. The

Presidential Medal of Freedom, which was presented to me just yesterday by Libby during a celebration on Acme's rooftop garden, holds that spot.

It's a pretty piece of jewelry. I just wish I hadn't taken a bullet to the gut to get it.

***

EVE PHONES ME. "Donna, I know you're still recuperating..." She sighs. "But... well, you never got around to choosing your bridesmaid dress. And since the wedding is tomorrow..." Her voice trails off.

Oh, heck! With the mission, I'd forgotten all about it. And because of my injury and recuperation, Eve has graciously let it slide.

I can't let her down. "Eve, please forgive me! If it's convenient, I'll come right over."

"Thank you! I'll tell Security to let you right in. And Lee is tied up on donor phone calls so we shouldn't be disturbed."

"On my way," I assure her.

Hopefully, I'll be gone before Lee finishes up. Other than a visit he made with Eve to my hospital room, we haven't seen let alone talked to each other since the mission ended. Having been coerced into making the fake sex video has put a damper on our relationship. Being coerced into the same bed made the whole incident too real—at least, for Lee.

Sure, I get it: *awkward.*

But since there was no penetration, you'd think we'd be able to put the incident behind us, especially since the thumb drive of the video is at the bottom of the sea with Wilbur.

I pass on Mary's offer to drive me up to Lion's Lair. "The walk will do me good," I explain.

My wound aches as I make the uphill stroll, but it's worth the effort. From Hilldale's highest vantage point, the view of the Pacific Ocean is spectacular.

I reach Lion Lair's gate just as an overnight express truck pulls up. One of Lee's Secret Service agents puts it through the usual security protocols: for explosives, poisons, toxins, you name it. It passes with flying colors.

The agent who walks it to the door recognizes me. Knowing of my injury, he asks how I'm doing. "Could be better," I admit. "But it's great to be alive."

He nods. "I hear you."

Eve greets me at the door with fingers crossed. "I hope you love your choices."

"You've got excellent taste, so I'm sure I will."

The Secret Service Agent hands her the package.

"For Mr. Chiffray?" she asks.

"No, m'am. This one is addressed to you."

"Ah! Probably something I ordered for the wedding." She looks down at it. Then her eyes open wide. "*Hmm.* Looks official, so I guess it's not." She sighs. "Donna, I've laid out your dresses in the first downstairs bedroom on the right. Go ahead and start. I'll join you as soon as I can." She points down the hall.

"No problem. See you in a bit."

The bedroom shares the hall with Lee's office. He's on the phone so I feel no reason to let my presence be known.

As for the bridesmaid dresses, my choices are many and

all are beautiful. Each gown is a different cut, but all are the same bottle green color.

I'm in the process of zipping up the second dress when I hear a knock on the door. I assume it's Eve. Still facing the mirror, I say, "Hey, do you mind helping me with this zipper? With my injury, it's just out of reach."

"Ah! ...Sure, okay."

Oh, heck! It's Lee. Despite his obvious embarrassment, he comes over.

And that's how Eve finds us: *in zipper delicto.*

And why she drops what she holds in her hand: a thumb drive and photos—which, I assume, are in the video she'd find on it:

Of Lee and me, standing together, in each other's arms, and naked.

And another of us in bed, naked and entangled in each other's arms.

But the pièce de résistance is a swath of a sheet that flutters to the floor. I could guess what made its visible stain, but I don't have to, since a DNA analysis is also included.

Lee is too stunned to say anything. All he can do is sit.

And stare. And then cry into his hands.

It dawns on me: The same package will be delivered to Jack.

As fast as I can, I run out of the house and down the hill.

WHEN I WALK into the house, Jack is waiting for me.

He's not smiling. For that matter, he won't even look at me. Not when what he holds in his hand mesmerizes him:

A swath of sheet around the same size as what arrived for Eve. The DNA report has also been duplicated. So have the photo stills made from the video that recorded the blackmail.

When he finally lifts his eyes to me, his voice is devoid of all emotion.

I put my hand on his. "It's not what you think."

"Are you kidding me? It's exactly what I think—despite your bullshit confession!" Tossing my hand off, Jack stalks the room.

I beckon to the door. "The sooner Lee and I explain, the sooner Eve and he can get on with their lives, and we can do the same."

"Great. Let's get this over with once and for all." He slams the door on his way out.

There's nothing I can do but follow.

THERE WE SIT, the four of us. Jack is scowling. Eve is hollow-eyed.

Lee is bereft.

In time, Jack says, "You lied. You said you and Lee faked it. That he never, um, rose to the occasion."

"I knew the news that Lee ejaculated would upset you. You're proving it now."

"I think that I...that *Eve* and I—have a right to be pissed!" Jack retorts.

Eve cringes, but she doesn't look up.

"Considering the circumstances, we knew we'd have to

fake it. So, I took a liquid soap container into the bed with us to pass it off as...the real thing."

Jack snorts. "Yeah, right."

"She's telling you the truth now!" Lee exclaims.

"Only because your smut tape surfaced," Jack argues. "Okay, let's say I believe you—that Lee couldn't help himself around his favorite wet dream."

I'd slap him, but I want to see where this is going.

"I warned you that this would happen," he continues. "Despite POTUS's poll numbers being sky high, the video's release will make her a joke—and Lee too. Or Russia will blackmail you spy on her and to influence her decisions—"

"I'd never do that! I'll ...I'll have to withdraw from the ticket." Lee's voice cracks at the thought.

Realizing he's right, the room goes silent.

"Then the terrorists win," Eve declares. "Instead, why not get ahead of it?"

All heads turn to her. "It's the only way to minimize it," she continues. "First of all, 'Ruby Spencer' doesn't really exist. And even if she did, it's now assumed she and Aiden died in the fire."

I nod. "Eve has a point."

"And for that matter, the video could have been made at any time. Remember, Lee has been a handsome, rich, desirable, and *single* bachelor for quite some time—since his last day as POTUS, in fact. Some may say it's a miracle that more sex videos featuring him haven't surfaced. My guess: if he wasn't such a Boy Scout, there would have been." She rolls her eyes. "If this one ends up in the news tomorrow, will it ruin his reputation? Doubtful. It'll enhance his standing as a tech venture capitalist. My guess is it will also enhance his political ratings—and Libby's too."

"Bingo!" I declare.

Eve looks at her watch. "After tomorrow at sunset, 'Bachelor Lee' will be off the market. And with his adoring wife at his side, male voters won't hate him just because their wives find him swoon worthy. They'll think the stud found the one woman who can make him happy."

Lee gazes up at her. "You still adore me?"

Eve sighs. "I wouldn't be marrying you if I didn't."

"And you're right. I'm happiest when you're beside me," Lee replies.

The fervor in his voice brings tears to Eve's eyes. "Lee, darling, I certainly wouldn't have put up with your mooning after Donna all these years if I didn't think you'd one day come to your senses and realize you can't live without me."

"You're right," Lee marvels. "I can't."

I poke Jack. "Told you."

Eve strokes Lee's cheek. "I know, my darling Lee. Just like Donna can't live without Jack. She loves him with all her heart—and always will." Eve's eyes shift to Jack. "You know it too. So, quit doubting it! With all she—and you—have been through together, she doesn't deserve to be second-guessed on who she loves. If she can put up with what *you* must do in your line of work, then you can certainly put up with hers too—specifically, what Lee and she had to do when they thought your life was in danger. Otherwise, it's time you get out of diplomatic espionage altogether." Eve rises. "Now, if the Craigs will excuse us, Lee and I have a wedding to prepare for." She turns to me: "You're still going to be a bridesmaid, I hope?"

"Of course." My tight hug to her confirms it.

"Great." She looks at Jack. "And I assume you're still going to be Lee's best man?"

"Yes... If he'll still have me." I've never seen Jack so bashful.

Lee shakes his hand and then takes something out of his pocket: a ring box. "Then you'll need this when the time comes."

Jack opens it—and gawks. "Jeez! It's the twin of the Hope diamond! Next to it, Donna's ring is a... a microchip!" He kisses Eve's cheek. "You're a very lucky lady."

She chuckles. "No—Lee is a very lucky man."

"And don't I know it." Lee couldn't be more fervent.

They're still kissing as we head out the door.

I've filled Jack's arms with the bridesmaid dresses. He'll have so much fun zipping me in and out of them.

THE WEDDING of this former president who also happens to be one of the richest men in the world as well as the current president's running mate is everything you'd imagine: intimate, elegant, and informal despite a worldly guest list of movers and shakers.

I know its orchestration is all Eve's doing.

I'm so happy that Lee finally realizes that not only he needs her but how much he loves her.

Libby officiated. Her makeup artist did a wonderful job of covering any facial bruises. Eve had offered to arrange for an elevated chair. Instead, a bouquet-bowered podium allowed Libby to stand upright without crutches.

And now, hand in hand, the bride and groom meanders among their guests.

Trisha finds me in the best people-watching perch: the veranda overlooking the pool. From there, the crowd—men in tuxes and women in sparkling gowns—ebb and flow like human waves.

"Wow, Mom! Isn't it cool that Janie and you both got to be Eve's bridesmaids?" There is just a tinge of jealousy in her voice.

"I would have gladly traded places with you," I admit.

Trisha smiles at my loyalty but shakes her head. "Even if you'd offered, I wouldn't have let you—and neither would Dad."

"Goodness! What makes you say that?"

"Haven't you noticed? Of everyone here—and that includes Eve—he's the happiest about them finally tying the knot."

As I blush, she chuckles. "It's true, you know! Mary, Jeff, Evan, and I are Dad's everything. But he only has us because he fell in love with you, first and foremost." Trisha giggles. "Can you believe he was silly enough to think you liked Lee more?"

"You know about that? ... How?"

"Duh! He's such a typical guy! You know: all tough on the outside, but a scared little boy on the inside." She leans in. "But don't let him know I'm on to him, okay? I've still got a couple of years here at the old homestead and I can use that to my advantage."

"Not too often, I hope."

"If you say so." She crosses her heart. And then she giggles.

So do I. Talk about a chip off the old block: mine.

At that moment, Jack looks over. Our joy only widens his grin.

I wave back, but then I nod toward the front gate.

He gets the message: if we slip out now, we won't be missed.

Trisha kisses me goodbye. "Don't wait up," she teases.

I raise a brow. "You bet I will."

"No more." Jack's vow comes out in a whisper.

We're outside Lion's Lair's gates. To this point, neither he nor I had said a word. From this vantage point, the ocean truly does seem endless.

"No more what?" Just as the question leaves my lips, I dread having asked it.

No more trusting me—even after Eve's startling yet stark assessment of Jack's unnecessary insecurities?

No more Acme—which tests our love in every way, only to reaffirm the strength of our devotion—not only to each other, but to our country?

No more us—despite the undying desire we feel for each other every waking moment?

He stares at me, as if I should already know the answer:

I do. And I say it out loud: "No more doubts."

We seal our vow with a kiss.

THE END

Other Books by Josie Brown

The Extracurricular Series

I Followed My Heart to You (Book 1)

And Then You Broke My Heart (Book 2)

I Love You with All My Heart (Book 3)

The Totlandia Series

Adorable You (Book 1)

Because of You (Book 2)

After You (Book 3)

Always You (Book 4)

Beautiful You (Book 5)

Without You (Book 6)

Dearest You (Book 7)

Forever You (Book 8)

The True Hollywood Lies Series

Hollywood Hunk

Hollywood Whore

More Josie Brown Novels

The Candidate

Secret Lives of Husbands and Wives

The Baby Planner

How to Reach Josie

To write Josie, go to:
mailfromjosie@gmail.com

To find out more about Josie, or to get on her eLetter list for book launch announcements, go to her website:
www.JosieBrown.com

You can also find her at:

www.AuthorProvocateur.com

twitter.com/JosieBrownCA

facebook.com/josiebrownauthor

pinterest.com/josiebrownca

instagram.com/josiebrownnovels

josiebrown.bsky.social

www.ingramcontent.com/pod-product-compliance
Lightning Source LLC
Chambersburg PA
CBHW072104300726
48975CB00003B/697